I.C.U.

I.C.U.

Al Kirkland

ISBN: Softcover 978-1-4257-7320-5

This is a work of fiction. Names, characters, places and incidents either are the product of the author's imagination or are used fictitiously, and any resemblance to any actual persons, living or dead, events, or locales is entirely coincidental.

This book was printed in the United States of America.

To order additional copies of this book, contact:
Xlibris Corporation
1-888-795-4274
www.Xlibris.com
Orders@Xlibris.com
40863

CONTENTS

CHAPTER 1

The loud gangster rap music did not filter out the banging on Darell's bedroom door. *Boom! Boom! Boom!* were the sounds Darell heard but choose to ignore. His thoughts were on his eighteenth birthday tomorrow, and his high school graduation, on the same day. He felt as though tomorrow was a beginning of a new life for him, from boyhood to manhood. *Boom! Boom! Boom!* This banging was much louder, and much harder than the usual knocks and bangs that his mom usually made to get his attention. The banging was much higher too! "Maybe she done got her weight up and gotten a little stronger," he thought to himself. But he knows that she is mad or maybe furious at him, for letting the trash truck leave without him taking out the overflowing trash bag in the kitchen. Because Darell and his mother are the only two living at her house, he feels as though if he doesn't do what she tells him to do in the house, then she should do it. Darell wasn't worried about his mom coming into his room, because the bolt lock on the door prevented that from happening.

Boom! Boom! Boom! Boom! Boom! These thundering sounds were pounding on the bedroom door. "Police! I'll tear it down if you don't open it!" This masculine voice was definitely not his mother's. Darell stared at the door wondering what illegal activity he had done and who told on him. He already had his alibi, as he always say, "I was with June Bug and Ray-Ray and dem" (his boys in the hood). As soon as he unlocked the dead bolted door, the six foot seven 270-pound police officer named Tiny, pushed Darell and the door back as he barged in.

"Turn the music off!" Officer Tiny growled. Darell was too shocked to move. Tiny walked over to the stereo and ripped the plug from the socket as his partner Ricky walked in the bedroom smiling. Ricky was a nineteen-year-old rookie on the force who has younger brothers living with his mom at his mother's house that act the same way that Darell was acting. They just lay up and chill all day to music and drinking forty-ounce beers.

"What's up, yo?" Ricky says to Darell. "Your mom wants you to leave, yo. And she said that I can rent this room, yo." Ricky walked over to the bed and removed the sheet from it and said, "I hope you do not wet the bed. You don't wet the bed do you, yo?"

"Take what you're going to wear 'now'. You gots to go." Tiny said as he opened the closet door.

"Where I'm going? What do you mean my mom wants me out of the house? I ain't do nothing."

Darell's mom shouted from the hallway, "That's why you got to go. You do not do anything around here. I am sick and tired of reminding you what I told you to do. You'll be eighteen tomorrow. Go get your own house and live the way you want to live."

Tiny pulled a pair of jean pants off a hanger in the closet and threw them on the bed. He grabbed the belt from the closet, and then threw it back in the closet, on the floor. "You don't need no belts. You like to let your pants sag." Tiny walked away from the closet and asked, "Where's your T-shirts? Where's your white tees at?" he asked as he opened the dresser drawer. After throwing two white T-shirts on the bed, Tiny pointed at Darell's boots and asked, "Are you taking them boots with you?"

"I'll come back and get them," Darell told the officer.

"See. You're hardheaded." Tiny told him as he snatched the fan from the window. "You're not coming back." Officer Tiny picked the pair of Timb's up and threw them out of the bedroom window.

"Yo, dog, you gots to go. Those some nice Timb's he threw out the window. Somebody might walk by and get them boots," Officer Ricky told him.

Darell ran to the window and yelled at Tiny, "How you just going to throw my boots outside. I told you I was coming back."

Tiny grabbed Darell by his neck and said, "You can get thrown out there, too. Now which way do you want to leave?" Darell was gasping for air as he tried to pull the officer's hand from around his neck. "Huh? Which way do you want to go?" Darell pointed at the door as he tried to breathe. The officer pushed him away from him and said, "Well, get!" Darell walked out of the room crying, feeling embarrassed. His pseudo-intellectual street knowledge allowed him to explain to the officers about the law that all of the kids have learned in school.

"DYFS said that if parents have issues with kids they have to resolve it in court. Y'all just can't kick me out of the house. That's illegal, yo."

Officer Ricky smiled at Darell and said, "Your mom made a complaint to us saying you threatened her. Under the Domestic Violence Act that justifies your removal from home, Yo."

Darell walked down the stairs with the officers following him. "I ain't threatening her. She hit me. She hit me on my arm."

"You raised your balled up fist at me like you wanted to hit me. You should be glad I called the cops. Next time you raise your hand up at me I'm just going to do what I gotta do. That way I ain't got to worry about you no more."

"That's a threat. Isn't that a threat right there? Didn't she just threaten me?"

Darell looked at officer Ricky with his eyes wide open, as if her statement was probable cause for her to get kicked out of the house too. Officer Ricky shook his head at Darell and said, "That's a statement, not a threat."

"Mom, what's this officer talking about moving into my room? How's he's going to just move into my room?"

"This is my house," she snapped back, "Do you pay rent here? Do you give me money for anything in here? If I want to move somebody into your room, I will move them in. You'll be a grown man tomorrow. Go get you a room and a job. I don't have time for this. I'm too blessed to be stressed." She walked over to let Joe, the neighborhood maintenance man, in the house. Joe had the new doorknobs for the front and back doors.

Darell thought of a way to solve the whole problem. He walked to the kitchen, grabbed a trash bag from the cabinet and started to change the kitchen trash bag that was full to the top with trash on the floor all around it.

"Don't touch the trash now! It's too late for that. The garbage truck left already. I'll get someone to take out the trash," his mom said.

"Who's gonna take the trash out then?" he asked.

"Don't worry about it. Officers, can you escort him out of my house?" she said as she walked upstairs.

"Wait a minute. Wait a minute. Time out!" Darell said as he motioned his hand in the sign of a T.

"Oh, you done got it all twisted, young man," Officer Tiny said. "You see, with your mom it's time out. But when the police comes, it's time up. You gots to go."

Officer Ricky smiled at Darell and said, "Don't worry about the trash, yo. I'll be taking out all of the trash now," he said sarcastically. "And the first piece of trash that gots to go is you, yo."

Feeling embarrassed and humiliated, Darell put his head down and walked out the back door crying. He picked his boots up from the ground and stared at his opened bedroom window.

Officer Tiny explained to him that the best thing to do was to give his mom some time and give her a call later.

"If you go back into that house without a police escort or without her permission that's unlawful entry. That's about the same as a B and E charge, Breaking and Entering. You get three years in prison for that, son. And if I get a call to come back here and get you out again, it's going to be nothing nice when you leave."

Officer Ricky raised his eyebrow and smiled at Darell and said to him, "Three years is just about enough time to allow me to move from the back bedroom to the front bedroom, yo! By that time, I'd been done have a ring on your mom's finger and she'll have my last name too! And if you choose to come back, you can take my trash out and cut my grass too, yo!"

Darell smacked his lips and took a deep breath before walking away. He decided to call his father in which he knew his father would be telling him, a lot of "I told you so's." But since he's graduating tomorrow, he thought maybe his father would have a little heart and allow him to move in with him. Darell thought DYFS taught him well. And being kicked out of your mother's house is what happens to other people. Now he has to deal with it.

After contacting his father, they met at a restaurant across the street from New Jersey's most notorious State Prison. They sat and ate burgers and fries, and talked about his mom and the responsibilities of being a man. Darell's father, John, anticipated Darell's graduation from high school, so he bought Darell a graduation gift for Darell's achievement. John purchased a new S-Class Benz with twenty-inch chrome rims online and had it delivered to him. He parked it in the back of the prison's parking lot. He wanted this to be the closest Darell got to this or any prison as long as he's still alive. John always told Darell, "As long as I'm alive, don't let me visit you in prison. I don't want you to be inside of a place looking at something that you can't get to." This brand new Benz will definitely draw attention in the neighborhood. This graduation gift is just what he needed to uphold his image as a man tomorrow when he turns eighteen years old. Darell sat with his father in the fast food restaurant as his father talked to him, looking at his father as if it wasn't his fault he got kicked out of the house.

"I told you how your mom was. But I blame you for this. You're the man of the house. Anything physical that has to be done in there, you should do it. And if you don't see anything that needs to be done, then you should've asked her if there was anything that needed to be done."

"But she always wants me to do something."

"Then you should always do something. Don't she cook and feed you? And don't she give you money for your pocket when you need it?"

"Yeah, she be looking out. But she always be getting mad at me for no reason."

"It's probably because you don't be doing what she wants you to do. And now she's just fed up with you. If it was me, I'd been done hooked off on you and kicked you out of the house myself. It's good that she's done it now. Because when you get grown, it only gets worse."

Darell is now confused about being a man at eighteen. "Maybe eighteen is the start of the new revolution for young men," he thought.

"Your mom is probably really mad at me. But since her and I aren't together, she takes it out on you. But you don't make it no easier for her by acting the way that you do."

"Dad, I'm just being me."

"The problem is that you don't know who you are. You're a boy trying to be a man. You have to represent me when you're at home and in the streets. When people see you they see me. Until that crazy side comes out of you. See, that's your mom there. That's not me."

"She wants me to think about what she wants me to do without her even telling me. I don't read minds."

"Well I don't know about that. But maybe you need to stay one step ahead of her. Let her know that you're trying." His father looked at the boots Darell placed underneath the table and asked, "What's with the Timb's?"

"The police threw them out my bedroom window. The cop said that he's moving into my room. Talking about I'm going to be cutting his grass and taking his trash out."

"That's to let you know that if you're going to be the man of the house and you don't live up to it, somebody else will. That cop ain't moving in that house. Those boots you got. You're only supposed to wear them when it rains or if there's snow on the ground. See what I'm wearing (pointing at his feet). Gators. Alligators or crocodiles, that's all I wear. And when you wear shoes they should always be shining. A man's shoe should always be shining when he walks. You feel me?"

"I ain't got no shoes. But I'll shine up my sneakers when I get a chance."

"You'll be a man tomorrow so start acting like one. Get you a job and get some shoes and stop sagging your pants. Put a belt on. You look like a thug. You ain't gang banging are you?"

"Naw. That's not me."

"All right, get you a young lady. Spend some time with her and do some traveling. Every lady that you see on the street, treat her with respect. You know, say hello to her and say nice things to her, too."

After they ate John stood up, emptied the tray in the can, and told Darell, "Let's go." They walked through the parking lot and onto the sidewalk.

Darell asked, "Where's your car?"

"I'm not driving my car today. He pulled out the keys to the Benz and told Darell, "I drove your car." He handed over the keys to the Benz and said, "We'll walk over to it. It's on the other side of town. The car is brand new and black, with chrome rims on it." John found himself talking and walking by himself for the moment. Darell stood still in shock.

"Come on. This is your graduation gift. You made the effort to get your diploma. So I made the effort to get you something to drive in. See if you're really determined to do it you can only do it with determination."

They shook hands and hugged. John congratulated his son and gave him the extra set of keys. "This should be your last long walk into manhood." John didn't tell him that the car was inside of the prison's parking lot all the way in the back. He told him it was on the other side of town so Darell wouldn't notice it as they approached it.

As they crossed the street from the restaurant, two men walked toward them smiling. Terry (the neighborhood thug) asked John, "You got a dollar I can have?"

John told him, "I need mine," and kept walking by the two men. Terry pulled out a gun from his waist and turned toward John and said, "I need yours, too," as he pointed the gun sideways at John's head.

Darell was surprised at how bold this man could be, to rob somebody in broad daylight at two o'clock in the afternoon.

"Oh, this is how you get paid, huh?" John asked him.

"Don't worry about how I get mines, just give it up." Terry told him as he walked closer to him. Terry's partner noticed that they were getting some attention from cars that were passing by. And he knew that it was shift change for the officers at the prison, so he wanted to make this robbery as quick as possible.

"Hold your arms up higher," Terry's partner told John as he attempted to reach in his pocket. John punched the robber in the face, knocking him to the ground. Terry took one step away from John. *Bang! Bang!* Two slugs hit John in the chest. Terry pointed the gun at Darell and stared at him. John took two steps toward Terry before collapsing to the ground.

Darell took one step toward Terry with his fist balled up and a face full of anger.

Terry's partner got up from the ground and ran. Terry backed away from Darell as he panicked and ran into the street. Darell ran after him as he watched a sports van driven by a corrections officer who just got off from work hit Terry, knocking him seven feet into the air. When Terry fell to the ground, Darell thought about his father. He ran back to his father to assist him as his father lay on his back.

"Somebody call an ambulance! Somebody call an ambulance!" Darell shouted. In the midst of all this commotion everyone reached for their cell phones. The neighbor, bystander, and people in view of the cars passing by called 911. Some reported a robbery in progress. Some reported someone got shot. While Darell was kneeling down holding his father trying to comfort him, some people called 911 stating that he was robbing the man.

The corrections officer who hit Terry thought he killed him because of the excess speed he was traveling. "I didn't see him! I didn't see him! He just ran right out in front of me. He was running. I didn't see him," the officer said out loud as he panicked. He called 911 complaining about how Darell was chasing Terry who ran in front of his car.

"Shots fired" was heard on the police radio, with the location indicated. That announcement superseded all other calls on the police radio. When officers hear "Shots fired" on the radio they respond to that location like a boulder falling hard on something soft. They're ready to smash anything or anybody that looks out of place or gets in their way.

An eight-year-old boy who walked by the accident picked up Terry's gun that landed by a car tire twenty feet away. He first thought that it was a toy gun that someone threw away.

The corrections officer glanced at Darell and his father and noticed the blood on his father's shirt. He thought, maybe the man on the ground got stabbed and the man that he hit ran to prevent from getting stabbed.

The corrections officer heard the noise of the sirens getting closer as he stared at Darell to see if he was robbing the man he was holding. The eight-year-old boy looked at the officer's uniform and noticed that he wasn't carrying a gun. He thought that the gun he found probably belonged to the corrections officer, thinking that the officer might have dropped it in the commotion.

As the police and ambulance were arriving at the scene, the corrections officer turned toward the man he hit, only to see this boy with the gun and his finger on the trigger, pointing it at him. The officer was lost for words until he heard the boy utter something as the boy walked toward him.

With the sirens in the background, the boys words of "I found this on the ground," was not fully heard by the officer. "On the ground!" was all the corrections officer understood as the boy spoke. He thought that the man across the street must have been shot by this little boy.

"Don't shoot! I didn't mean to hit him. I didn't see him," the corrections officer said as he backed up with both of his hands above his head.

"I found this on the ground," the boy said as he raised the gun higher pointing it at the officer's head, as he tried to hand the gun to him, with the noise of the sirens blaring.

Darell is looking at this situation while holding onto his father. The police officers arrived with different versions to this incident by the numerous phone calls they received. The corrections officer began to kneel down with his hands still up. The first cop that arrived, saw the boy with the gun, and parked his patrol car next to Darell and his father. Thinking that they were the victims and the shooter still had the gun. The police pulled their guns out and pointed them at the boy.

"Freeze and drop your weapon!" the police shouted. "Don't move. Drop it," another officer shouted. Darell lowered his father out of his arms and on to the ground. He wanted to explain to the officers what was going on.

"It's not mine. It's not mine. I found it!" the boy cried out as he looked at the twelve gauge shotguns and handguns pointing at him.

"No. Hold it. Wait. Wait!" Darell said out loud to all of the officers as he ran toward them. The boy decided to give the gun to the police. He pointed the gun away from the corrections officer and pointed it at the police to give it to one of them.

One policeman realized that his partner might get shot by this boy, so he leaned closer to the boy to blow him away with the twelve gauge shotgun.

Darell ran to the officer and pushed the gun upward. *Boom!* One round from the gun went off into the air. The boy dropped the gun and ran out of fright. One officer shouted, "Get him!"

Before Darell could explain to the officer what had happened, the officer pulled the shotgun from his hands and hit Darell in the mouth with the back of the gun, knocking him to the ground. The other officers responded to this situation with force also.

"Lay down. On your face. On your face. Now!"

Darell thought about his father and tried to crawl to him. One officer kicked him in the ribs and another officer put his foot on Darell's back pushing him down with his foot. "Don't move," the officer told him as he pointed the shotgun at Darell's head. They cuffed him and placed him into the patrol car that was next to his father who was still lying on the ground. His view of his father was blocked by medics and officers that were surrounding him. With his mouth bleeding and windows rolled up, his account of the events couldn't be heard. Darell knew that his father was strong and with as many medics around him, he would survive.

The corrections officer was directing and calling all of the shots to make sure his victim was comfortable. He ran back and forth to the ambulance getting pillows and asking the robber, "Are you okay? Where do you hurt at? We're taking you to the hospital. Do you want some water? Get him some water. Y'all got water in that truck? Let's get him on the stretcher!"

One by one the medics walked away from Darell's father, and over to the robber. Darell was wondering what was taking them so long to put his father on the stretcher and to the hospital. He finally got a view of his father's legs. As the medics continue to walk away, he got a better view.

Finally, one of the medics took one of the blankets from the ambulance and walked back over to his father. The medic unfolded the blanket and began to cover his father's feet.

"Yeah, cover his body so he won't go into shock," Darell said to himself. "Why they ain't put him on the stretcher yet? Maybe the wound's not all that bad." The medics pulled the covers up to his father's knees, waist, chest, neck and up and over his father's head. "Noooo!" he cried as he shook his head from side to side.

The bystanders pointed at Darell as they talked to the police. The police took notes and charged Darell with murder and assaulting an officer, for grabbing the officer's gun.

The boy was placed into another car and charged with robbery and attempted robbery of a corrections officer.

After catering to the robber, the corrections officer helped to escort him over to the other ambulance next to the patrol car Darell was sitting in. The robber Terry acted as if he was in so much pain as he lay on the stretcher.

They rolled the man next to the back car window and stopped prior to putting Terry into the ambulance. Darell stopped crying as he stared at Terry. Terry's pain seemed to stop as he looked into the car and recognized Darell. Terry smiled at Darell and winked at him. Darell stared at him and watched them push Terry into the ambulance and drive away.

The next day, the police and the car insurance investigator were at the hospital trying to locate Terry. Terry was nowhere to be found. He told the nurse that he was going to the bathroom and limped out of the back door early the next morning. So the detective decided to talk to Darell as he sat in the police lockup.

With swollen lips and bruised ribs he was reluctant to talk to anybody especially to those who caused his pain. Darell sat in a small room with no windows in it, staring at a two-way mirror. His T-shirt was covered with dry blood from the shotgun assault.

He was hoping by this time somebody done told the truth about the whole incident. The detective entered the room with a notebook in his hand hoping that Darell would confess to murdering his father. The more the detective talked, the more Darell's hope faded about someone telling the truth.

"I'm Detective Gardner and I'm assigned to your case. You are Darrow Steps. Dayrow Steps. Darell Steps. How do you pronounce your name? Da-rell Steps. That sounds like it," the detective said. "Darell Steps. That's your name, right?"

Darell nodded his head.

"You're charged with," he paused to look at the charges, "Well it looks like they threw the book at you and want you to read the book and pick out something you didn't do. You're charged with first degree murder, robbery, attempted murder, assaulting an officer, a whole lot of gun possessions, endangering the welfare of a minor, disorderly conduct, resisting arrest," he paused for a few seconds and said, "Let's just make a deal. If you plead guilty I'll ask the prosecutor to just ask the judge to sentence you to fifty years in prison." He looked at Darell for a response. Darell sat motionless and stared at the mirror on the wall.

"I'm here to get a statement from you, Mr. Steps. You could make a phone call if you want to. We called your mom already. Do you have an attorney you could call?"

"No, I don't need an attorney."

"Okay, Mr. Steps. You have the right to remain silent. Anything you say may and will be used against you. You can stop answering questions at any time. Do you understand your rights? I looked for your rap sheet and found that you didn't have a police record. So this is your first offense." He continued to flip pages and said, "Here we are. You and your eight-year-old accomplice shot Mr. John Steps and attempted to rob Terry, before he ran across the street. We got the gun. The bullets match the slugs that Mr. Steps was shot with. Did you know Mr. Steps?" he asked, realizing that they had the same last name. The detective began to ask what might seem to be a pertinent question. "Did Mr. Steps owe you some money or something? Did y'all get into a dispute?"

Without looking at him Darell said to him, "He's my father."

Darell continued to look in the mirror as he talked. "I was walking with my pop. Two thugs tried to rob us. The one that got hit by the car had the gun. His partner tried to put his hand in my father's pocket. My pop dropped a right hand on him and knocked him to the ground. The thug with the gun shot my pop twice. I moved toward him and was about to drop him but he ran. A car hit him. The boy picked up the gun and tried to give it to the corrections officer. That's when your boys tried to shoot him. I pushed the gun away from the direction of the boy and the shotgun went off."

The detective tried to compare notes by reading from his notes. Nothing was adding up, as he realized that this whole situation has gotten twisted. He jumped up out of his seat and snatched the door open.

"Get his mom on the phone and see if she knows John Steps," he ordered the officer that was standing by the door outside the room.

"Put an APB (All Points Bulletin) out on this Terry guy. Drag him off the streets. If Mr. Steps is his father, drop all charges on him and the other kid and take him home." The detective walked back to the table and snatched his notebook from it. He now knows why Terry left the hospital so soon.

Within a week, Terry was captured. Darell was asked to come and identify him. The prosecutor made a deal with Terry after he was identified. The deal was for him to only serve fifteen years in prison, with a ten year stipulation. Terry was a known felon who knew how to jail. He knew the system and knew the streets well enough to stay on it. It was a good deal to only get a fifteen year prison sentence for murder. The average murder sentence is twenty-five years to life. Darell asked one of the street thugs he knew, how was that possible. "What you know, who you tell on and how you cooperate with the police determines how much time you serve in the criminal system", the thug told him.

This deal infuriated Darell. He wanted to snap and black out on somebody. He told his mom about the fifty year deal he was offered. Closure was near with his father's death. The funeral was heartfelt. He had a better bond with his mom, now the pain started all over again because he was mad at the system. He felt trapped and useless thinking that the system thought his father's life was useless if someone else killed him. "Fifty years if I kill him. Fifteen if someone else," he said as his mom stood in front of him, reflecting on her ex-husband.

His conversation with his father and the knowledge his father gave him on how to be a man taught him what he was feeling when he feels pain as a man. But fully understanding the feeling was difficult. Revenge was on his mind. He was vexed. He wanted to show his father that he was living the life of a man. Darell was under the impression that part of being a man is to do unto others as they do unto you. That was the street knowledge that he carried over from his adolescence. **Revenge.**

The smile and wink Terry gave him bothered him each time he saw an ambulance. The thought of Terry being in there smiling stayed on his mind. He just couldn't help but to imagine that he'd be getting patched up soon, but his father was the one that had to die. His attempt to find his car failed. He kept his car keys in front of his bedroom mirror. Darell felt that the keys weren't a souvenir, they were a part of his life. He even called every Benz car dealer in New York, New Jersey and Pennsylvania. He thought Terry knew where the car was and followed his father to car jack him for it. But asking Terry where the car was, was not possible. "Just ain't happening," he thought.

Darell found Terry's place of residence in state facilities by looking on the inmate indicator web site. "I should get him," was his thought each day until he got used to saying it. He didn't want to wait fifteen years but didn't know what to do. "I'm gonna get him," sounded more comfortable to him. So he decided to act on it. That made him more determined to find Terry to do unto others so that he could find closure. He wanted Terry to suffer the way his father suffered before he died. Boldness and a strong determination gave him the heart to walk to New Jersey's most notorious prison: Trenton State. With his weapon tucked in his waist, he entered the prison's lobby for a visit with Terry.

Officers at the prison informed him Terry had to put him on his visitor's list before he could visit. He realized then that the residents are well-fed and well-protected at New Jersey's finest prison. "Anything is possible if you're determined," were the words of his father. "You can only do it with determination," he remembered his father saying.

Out of all of the criminals and ex-convicts in the neighborhood he talked to, no one had the insight on how to get in and out of a maximum prison for a short period of time.

"It's not like the city lockup, where you stay for a couple of weeks or years. You're talking about Trenton State Prison," the neighborhood thief, Mudman, told him. "I did years in Trenton, Rahway Prison, and Leesburg." Mudman, a career criminal who always got locked up for petty crimes continued, "Unless you're a visitor to see a convict, you ain't going inside no prison just because you want to see somebody. You got to be charged with a crime. And to get to Trenton Prison, you got to do about ten years or more. Ask Father Time, he'll tell you."

CHAPTER 2

Father Time lived two doors away from Darell. He's an ex-convict who was a known rebel in Wilbur Section in Trenton, New Jersey. The majority of his life was behind bars in just about every prison in New Jersey. At the age of ten, he entered the juvenile institution at the reform school for boys in central New Jersey. Now at the age of seventy-six, he is paroled from Trenton State after doing fifty-six years there. Father Time has been paroled almost a year now. He lives with his daughter but confines himself to his bedroom as if he is still institutionalized.

Darell seldom saw Father Time. Some days he would see him taking the trash out in the mornings before he went to school. He overheard his daughter telling his mother about his drinking problem. Moonshine whiskey was his favorite. Every now and then a bottle of it would get snuck in the back door. Drinking is not allowed in her house. This back door passage was blocked when his daughter smelled alcohol on his breath, so she boarded up the door with nails. Darell wanted to talk to him without his daughter in the house. He brought a bottle of that watered down moonshine from the corner liquor store and waited for the next day. Although his feet or what he calls his dogs prevented him from walking too much, Father Time still takes out the trash.

The next morning, Darell took his trash can to the sidewalk in front of his house and waited for Father Time. Darell wasn't interested in Father Time's real name. His opportunity to meet him came when Father Time and his daughter walked out together and she got into a cab. Darell ran back into the house to get the moonshine so that he could greet him right. When Father Time walked back into the house, Darrell decided to knock on the front door. Father Time opened the door and recognized that Darell was the one that always played what he called "that boom-boom music."

After introducing himself to Father Time, Darell asked him, "Is this whiskey the same as that down south moonshine whiskey?" Father Time looked at the bottle and reached for it. Darell walked inside the house and handed him the bottle.

"No," he said as he reminisced about the way they make it in the deep woods of Louisiana. "This is like that funny drink Kool-Aid. It got a lot of sugar in it. This is what you drink?" Darell wasn't an amateur to drinking whiskey, but he preferred to drink forty ounce beers.

"No, I just bought the bottle to see how it tasted. Should I drink it straight or with ice or mix it with something?"

"I drink mine's straight young man".

"It's not too early in the morning to be drinking, is it?"

Father Time's eyes lit up. "No. No. No. Come here. I'll get you a glass."

They sat down drinking and talking about each other and the neighborhood. When Father Time mentioned his prison life, Darell stayed on that subject.

It was either the cheap moonshine that made him talk, or the company. Father Time told his life story like a book. Prison life was so embedded in his life that prison slang was still in him as he talked. "Prison is real to some people, to others it's a joke. It's just a place to jail. Prison ain't that much different from out here," Father Time said as he poured Darell a small glass of moonshine, and took a long swig from the bottle. "Everything that's out here is in there. So it ain't no different."

"If I wanted to go to prison to step to someone. You know, to hurt somebody," Darell asked cautiously, "How could I do it?"

"Prison is not like the housing projects. You can't just go there. The judge sends you there. Then the system determines which prison you go to." Darell hadn't tasted his drink yet, so he picked it up, smelled it and looked in the glass thinking that it looked just like water not Kool-Aid. "Father Time, what system are you talking about?"

"When you just get to prison they get the psychologist, the social workers and some of everybody to talk to you. They look on the paper, see your age and what type of crime you did. That's when they give you your points. Well you really got those points before you get there. But before you leave, they'll tell you what prison you're going to. You don't tell them what prison you want to go to; they tell you. If you're scared to go to the prison they're sending you to, you gotta tell them why you're scared."

Darell tasted the moonshine whiskey and started coughing. He frowned as he put down his drink and said, "This ain't no Kool-Aid!" as he continued to cough. He pushed the glass to the middle of the table, wiping his lips with his finger.

"Boy," Father Time said as he laughed, "You just don't know how to drink this." Father Time poured Darell's drink into his bottle.

"Well, let me ask you like this then," Darell said as he leaned forward in his chair. "This is farfetched, but I want you to think about it seriously and make the impossible possible."

Father Time took another long swig from the bottle. He coughed when he finished and said, "It's been a long time since I hit it like that, but I still knows how to hit it."

"Suppose you wanted to, let's say, get someone in prison that killed your daughter. What would you do to go after him?"

"I'd do a soft crime on the street, like steal a car or something, where someone don't get hurt."

"What would you do on the streets to get inside of Trenton State Prison?" Darell asked with excitement.

"If I stole a car they'd offer me a plea bargain deal. I would turn down the deal and they would probably give me five years. The first prison I'd get sent to would be a reception facility. Now this place is where they determine which prison they'll send you to. But to get to Trenton State Prison, you got to be doing twenty years or more. Unless, you're doing small time and get into a fight at that reception facility. Then they'll send you to Trenton State Prison." Father Time finished the moonshine by taking two more gulps from the bottle then wiped his lips with his hand. He told Darell, "That will hold me until you bring me some of the real moonshine whiskey."

"Mudman got sent to Trenton State from there after a guard said he assaulted him. The guard said that Mudman threw a little pack of pepper on him. That pepper ain't hurt nobody. Mudman just wanted to let the guard know how petty he was."

"So, Father Time, when you're in this place, this reception facility, and you throw a pack of pepper on a guard they'll send you to Trenton, even after they told you, you were going to another prison?"

"In a heartbeat. It could be a punch, a pack of pepper, salt, sugar or anything. You can throw some water on him. That's an assault. You go straight to Trenton State. No questions asked. But see, now you be doing lockup time for a few days for assaulting an officer. After that you'll finish up the rest of your time like a man, or until someone made you their woman. They say when you first get to prison, punch the toughest convict in there. They would do that just to let the other prisoners know that their willing and ready to fight. And that they're tough too."

"But the one that gets punched, might not have to fight back. He might be the one doing a double life sentence, plus two hundred years. He'll get somebody else to do his dirty work. That's the scary part of it. You'll never know when it's coming. I had some rough days in Trenton State. But to get there without committing a hard crime with some years to it, assault somebody at the reception facility. That's the express way to Trenton State."

Darell left Father Time's house feeling disappointed. All of that prison talk scared him, and made him realize why his father didn't want him in there. He reached a conclusion with himself that a fifteen year wait might be a better choice.

Days and weeks went by with Darell feeling agitated, frustrated, and angry at anything and everything. Darell passed his driver's test and received a license to drive. This license eased his pain a little, until he thought about his car. He knew that he had a car, but couldn't find it. Asking the police to find it was like asking them to do him a favor, he thought. He got beat up by the police as he tried to be a hero. And his father's killer was living in prison, not feeling the pain and frustration Darell's feeling. He searched throughout the city for his car, knowing that it's parked somewhere on the streets of Trenton. Darell thought Terry probably knew where the car was, and stole the car when he left the hospital.

Working and trying to stay busy took his mind off the negative. But negative is what he always saw. While walking, he noticed a crime scene at a gas station across the street from his former high school. Detective Gardner drove in front of him at maximum speed with the lights flashing almost hitting him as he was walking. He ignored the yellow crime scene tape and drove right through it.

Not knowing who Darell was as he drove by him, Detective Gardner parked the car in the station to investigate the attempted robbery. As he walked toward the attendant with a small writing pad in his left hand, Darell approached him.

"You're Detective Gardner, right?" he said as he looked in the detective's face. "I'm Darell Steps. You know me from when my father got shot."

"Yeah. Yeah. I know who you are. What do you know about this robbery?" The detective barked at him as if Darell was somehow involved with it. "Did you see anything?"

"No. I just got here."

"Well, if you hear anything give me a call at the station."

"If I tell you who did it, will you give him a deal, too?"

"What? Don't worry about what I'll give him; just call me."

"You made me a deal. You thought I was guilty and wanted to give me fifty years."

"You're interfering with my police investigation. Leave the premises now!" The detective didn't want to respond to Darell's statement, so he walked away from Darell.

"What about the cop that kicked me? What ya'll gonna do about that?"

"I told you to leave. Don't let me have to lock you up." His threat irked Darell and caused him to walk away. Darell decided to irk him back but didn't know how. As he walked pass the detective's car, he noticed the box of doughnuts on the passenger's seat. The coffee cup was in the holder and the keys were in the ignition.

Darell wanted Gardner to notice him and to apologize for the mistreatment he suffered at the hands of the police. He thought as his father was dying, the officers were more concerned about catching his father's shooter than about his father's health. Darell decided to take Detective Gardner's patrol car and drive it to the police station. He knew once they caught him, he was going to go there anyway, so he wanted to have some fun as he went.

While Detective Gardner was investigating the crime scene, Darell got into the driver's seat, turned on the ignition, fastened the seat belt and drove away. He pushed every red button that was on the panel to activate every light and horn that was on the car.

As the siren blared, headlights flashed and the blow horn burst through the air, Darell sped out of the gas station.

"Hey! That's my car!" Detective Gardner shouted out to all officers at the scene. "Get him!" Detective Gardner announced on his radio to base, “Code 1046. Code 1046.” He got into the passenger’s seat of another patrol car. The driver of that patrol engaged in hot pursuit of his car. Darell drove toward his house to shake up the neighborhood drug dealers, before going to the police station. He drove to the corner of Monmouth and Locust Street, pulled up to the curb and asked the drug dealers, “Who’s selling weed?” One weed peddler was shocked and excited to see him driving a police car and shouted to Darell, “How’d you get that”? He started to get into the backseat of the car, but noticed the parade of police cars that were coming around the corner. Darell looked into the rearview mirror and told them, “I gotta bounce. I’ll holla at y’all later,” and drove off.

As he drove to the station, he heard on the police radio, “Base to all units. There is a weapon in the car. The perpetrator is to be considered armed and dangerous. Subject must be stopped by any means necessary. All unnecessary use of force is authorized.”

Darell picked up the police radio and said, “Base to Detective Gardner.”

“Detective Gardner. Go.”

Detective Gardner responded not knowing who was calling.

“Can I have one of these doughnuts?”

“You’ll get more than doughnuts when I catch you.”

The patrol cars tried to block him off but failed. Darell drove into the police stations parking lot and parked in the rear of the building. Other officers ran out of the building with their guns drawn, aiming at Darell. The officers driving behind him got out of their cars and swarmed around him pulling on the door handle.

When drivers lock their keys in the car and ask the police for assistance, Trenton Police never seem to have a shimmy with them. “Only traffic cops are allowed to have them,” they say. “We’re not authorized to use them, that’s why we don’t carry the shimmies.” That’s their excuse for not opening your car door for you.

About twenty cops rushed out of their patrol cars toward Darell with metal shimmies in their hands. They attempted to open the car door, but couldn't concentrate. They were too excited to get in.

As Detective Gardner stood at the driver's side door cussing at Darell, Darell turned up the volume on his favorite hip-hop station. The treble, bass and volume was up to the max. He signaled to Detective Gardner with a thumb's up sign, indicating to him that the doughnuts were the bomb, as he held one in his hand. Darell displayed this same doughnut to the other officers around the car, teasing them with it, while bobbing his head up and down with the music beats from the radio. He even grabbed the coffee from the holder and took a sip from the slit lid. Immediately, he spit out the contents of the cup on the floor and took the lid off the cup. After sniffing it, he realized that it was wine in the cup.

Curiosity allowed him to pull open the glove compartment in the car, only to find a small brown paper bag. Darell pulled a small bottle of wine from the bag, looked back at the detective and started to pour the wine from the bottle out too, but stopped. He decided to guzzle it down the way Father Time hit the moonshine bottle.

"If he touches that shotgun, shoot him!" Gardner said as he stood in front of the car.

Darell put the car in drive gear, put his left foot on the brake, and pushed the gas pedal all of the way down to the floor twice.

Va-rooom! Vroooooom! All of the officers that were near the car jumped back ten feet away from it and pulled out their guns.

"If that car moves one inch, open fire on him, and shoot until it stops!" Detective Gardner shouted.

Darell turned to look at all of the officers and laughed at all of them as he put the car back into park and took another drink from the bottle. He kept his finger on the lock button as the officer's tried to unlock the door. The music was too loud for him to hear the door unlock, plus the wine he drunk made Darell forget about pressing on the locked door button. As soon as he took his finger off of the lock button, all four doors were pulled open. Twelve hands grabbed Darell from all directions.

Three cops tried to pull him out of the front seat with the seat belt still attached to him. They put so much pressure on the driver's side door after opening it, the door broke off the hinges. The cops behind him in the back seat, tried to snatch him over the front seat. The officers in the front passenger's seat were pulling his right arm toward them.

One of the cops in the back seat pulled out a knife and cut the seat belt shoulder strap. After snatching him out of the car, Darell was escorted to the nearest hospital. When he returned back to the police station, there was no bail set for him. Darell's mom hired the neighborhood attorney to represent him. The attorney talked to Darell at the police station, knowing Darell had no win with this case. Darell was escorted into a small interview room where his attorney was waiting. He recognized Darell from the neighborhood on the block always walking with his pants sagging. Darell limped into the room with lumps and bruises on his face. After shaking Darell's hand, the attorney made Darell aware that he knew how he received the bruises on his face from what he was told by the police.

"The officer told me you hit your face on the car steering wheel." The attorney paused for a second, than he stated, "That's why you should always wear your seat belt when you drive."

Darell wasn't in any mood for talking, but he did tell him, "I was wearing my seat belt."

The attorney thought of a way to get paid more money from this case by asking, "Did the air bag inflate? Was there an air bag in the car? Was it defective, or something?"

Darell gave the attorney a disgusted look and told him, "I ain't hit my face on no car steering wheel."

"The officer said that . . ."

"And you believed them, too, huh? Whose side are you on . . . theirs or mines?"

The attorney looked confused as his lawsuit thought faded, knowing that someone was lying to him.

"Let's talk about my charges. What's my charges?"

"Well, you're charged with aggravated assault on a police officer."

"How much jail time do I get for that?"

"Well, you can get up to ten years for that."

"Can you make a plea bargain deal with them and try to get me less time than what they're trying to give me?"

The attorney smiled at Darell as he told him, "I did get you less time then what they are trying to give you. That's how good I am."

Darell felt a little better thinking that he had one of the best attorneys in the state. "What kind of deal did you make? How much time do I have to do for the aggravated assault charge?" Darell asked these questions with an ecstatic look on his face.

The attorney took a deep breath and told him, "Ten years in prison."

Darell didn't understand that double talk, it seemed confusing to him.

"How is doing ten years less than ten years?"

"You have nine counts of aggravated assault charges on you. Each count for each aggravated assault charge is ten years. So that's ninety years. Nine officers said that you punched them."

"What? I ain't punched nobody. They jumped on me!" Darell snapped at him.

"Plus you stole an official police car. That's fifteen years. And you have a lot of motor vehicle violations for careless driving, speeding, reckless driving, driving while intoxicated, and being a nuisance on the road." The attorney paused for a few seconds and told him, "If this is any consolation to you, the officers said they aren't charging you for stealing the doughnuts. They said the doughnuts were on the house. So they offered a plea bargain deal for ten years, but if you plead not guilty in court, they're trying to give you one hundred years in prison. What do you want to do?"

He pleaded guilty for numerous charges including traffic violations. He received a ten year sentence with a five year minimum.

If found guilty at a trial, he could have gotten close to a hundred years. His ten minutes of fame cost him his freedom. But it also allowed him his journey to his destination, Trenton State Prison.

CHAPTER 3

Two months after being sentenced to prison, Darell was transferred from the county jail to the state reception and assignment facility. This building is where the prison system determines what prison they'll be sending you to. It is on the grounds of the State Psychiatric Hospital surrounded by barbed wire and trees. When Darell saw the psychiatric hospital sign when entering the grounds, he figured they must have thought he was crazy for stealing a police car. "Maybe they're trying to figure out why I drove to the police station," he thought to himself.

After entering the building, corrections officers stripped him of all of his clothes and placed them in a box. They visually searched his body and told him to take a shower. After showering, he signed papers to send his clothes home, wondering if somebody would steal his boots.

"I never saw any Timb's like these before," was the usual saying when people looked at his boots.

The boots were made out of fiberglass, with gold colored sole bottoms. You could see right through the boot.

"Where did you get these from?" was the other usual question.

"I had them made like that" was his usual answer.

He received a gray jumper, and walked with shower shoes on his feet to a housing unit in the building. The next morning at 5:00 a.m., the wake up call was announced to take a shower again. After breakfast, all prisoners were hustled to another tier to live.

Darell felt lost in the new world of life behind bars. But he remembered what Father Time told him. "If you can live out here on the streets, then you can live in prison. Cause everything that's inside of prison came from out here." Darell's cell mate called himself Two-for-One. He lived in Camden, New Jersey before he got locked up. Any time he gave something of value out, you had to double that value back. He was a hustler on the streets in Camden. Now he was hustling in prison.

Two-for-One was the tier runner. He worked for the officer cleaning the tier. He had mad skills in everything. From cutting hair, buffing floors or fixing just about everything, Two-for-One did it all. After Darell walked into his cell, he bent over forward, with his back towards the cell door to place his personal property, into an empty plastic container. This container was protruding from underneath the bed next to another container that was full with commissary, and other necessities to survive in prison. Two-for-One walked into his cell as Darell was still bending over.

"The top bed is yours and the bottom one is me".

Darell turned towards him with his fist balled up and ready to swing. Two-for-one realized that he startled Darell, so he introduced himself to him. For about five minutes they didn't say another word to each other. Two-for-One was trying to figure him out. He wondered if they put Darell in number one cell because he was a minor or an informant.

"How old is you?" he asked Darell as he sat on his bed with a confused look on his face.

"I'm eighteen," Darell told him.

"Man, you look like you're fourteen-years-old. You got to get your weight up or something. Somebody might try you and take all of your goods. I'll try to look out for you as much as possible. But that all depends on what you're locked up for. Some inmates tell me that they sold drugs, robbed banks or shot at the police. Some even told me that they stole police cars. They must think

I'm a fool or something. Ain't nothing slow about me. He stared at Darell as he asked him, "What you locked up for?"

"For stealing a police car," After telling Two-for-One that, Darell walked to the back of the cell and stared out of the window. He never saw this part of Trenton before. This was an area of Trenton that he never ventured to. The outside scenery looked peaceful to him. He felt good knowing that he had a good view to look at. Two-for-One felt that Darell was lying to him and being facetious.

"Oh, you got jokes, huh? I think me and you are gonna have problems in here. You gonna learn the hard way what prison life is all about. I'll find out what you're in here for. Ain't no secrets in prison." Two-for-One stood up from his bunk and told the officer, "Let me out. I'm gonna get some ice. You want some ice, Officer?"

When the officer opened the cell door, Darell was told to step out of the cell too. He had to get processed through the batching system which was mandatory for all new inmates at this reception unit. This facility consisted of psychologists and social workers who would determine if inmates were crazy or had other special needs. The psychologist that Darell talked to looked crazy and deranged. His pants looked as if they hadn't been washed in three weeks. His hair was long and shaggy. And his shoes were dirty and dusty. Darell sat in the chair talking to the psychologist, thinking he was a far sight from what he pictured on TV. The psychologists on TV would have their clients lay down on a black couch. Darell sat on a wooden chair. He answered all of the psychologist's questions with an attitude. After ten minutes of questioning he asked the psychologist, "Where's your black couch? Are you a real psychologist?"

"I don't buy furniture for this institution. Are you uncomfortable in that chair, Mr. Steps?"

"It looks like you don't buy too many clothes, either. You're asking me too many questions. Ain't nothing wrong with me. Can I leave now?"

"Well, yes" he said as he put his ink pen up to his right ear. "We'll finish this conversation another time."

"I hope not. If I need you, I'll call you." Darell walked out of the room. Not knowing that this man could admit him to a psych ward in a mental hospital. After leaving the psychologist he sat in a room talking to a female social worker. They talked about his personal and family life. That made him feel a little more comfortable, so he continued to talk. She seemed like she cared and was concerned about him.

While Darell was away from his cell, his cell mate Two-for-One took advantage of the opportunity to view all of Darell's personal property. He came across the article about the police chase. He realized Darell was telling the truth about himself. When Darell returned from getting processed, a six-foot tall slim brown-skinned woman was waiting to talk to him. She was a social worker working for the department called Addiction Severity Index. She had a bright pretty smile, with two of the most beautiful eyes staring at him as he walked in the door.

"That's him," the officer said to her as he stood up. The officer directed them to a side room in the unit to talk privately. While sitting down in the room talking, Darell noticed her pretty feet. So he stared at them as they peeked from underneath the table. He was fascinated while looking at her pedicure, and wanted to ask her if he could massage her feet.

She noticed him looking at her feet and asked, "Is something wrong?" as she glanced down at her feet.

"No. I'm just thinking about something", he said as he smiled at her.

The social worker is sensitive about her appearance, so she demanded that he elaborate on his thoughts.

"I was just thinking earlier when I was looking out of the window, about what I'll not be seeing on the streets. But if I have never got locked up, I wouldn't have met a beautiful woman like you. I knew something good had to come out of all of this."

She thanked him for the compliment and said, “Now let’s talk about your drug problem.” Darell denied ever being addicted to drugs, but told her he’d tried just about all of them.

“What kind of drugs have you used?” Darell asked. She wanted to keep the conversation gangsta, and told him that this was not a social visit, but was for a drug prevention program. “Let’s try to keep this conversation about you. How or why did you stop smoking crack?”

Darell looked at her feet again to signal to her that he still wanted to inquire about her, then told her his crack history.

“I was in the hood with designer jeans, designer sneakers and designer boots. All of my outer gear was tight. I got a brand new Benz, and before I got locked up, I was going to add alligator and crocodile shoes to my wardrobe. When I hit that pipe, it was the best feeling in the world to me. But it made me feel bad afterwards. And all I wanted to do was to keep hitting it to feel good. So when I ran out of it, I felt bad and I wanted to cry.

“When I bought the crack, I told the guy that if it’s all of that, then I’ll be back. He said ‘You’ll be back’ as he smiled at me. He probably told his friends that he had me hooked, too. So I’m walking towards him on the blocks feeling like crying, because I needed more crack to feel better. As I was walking towards him, he noticed me coming and he started smiling. It was like he was saying, ‘Yeah, I got another one hooked.’ So I said to myself, the reason why I’m feeling bad, is because I’m making him feel good by buying this crack from him. So I decided to try to reverse this feeling. If I didn’t buy from him, maybe he wouldn’t be so happy. So as I walked towards him he smiled, reached in his pocket and said, ‘How was the rock?’ I turned to him and said, ‘It’s off the chain.’ I kept walking and that’s what I do to all crack dealers.”

“Did he ever try to sell you some more?”

“Yeah. He wanted to sell me some for half price to get me started again. I told him no because I was on my way to buy some shirts. When I told him that, he got an attitude with me. He said that I thought I was better than the rest of them. He said one day I will fall just like the rest of them. That's when I smiled at him knowing that he was upset and feeling bad because I wasn't hooked."

"That's good," she told him. "And I want to commend you for that." She took more information from him and determined that he didn't need to be in any drug program. When the interview was over, she stood up and shook his hand.

"Nice talking to you, and hopefully we can talk again when I get out."

She smiled at him and said, "Think about getting out first."

"Okay but you'll still be on my mind." He walked out of the room and back into his cell.

His cell mate Two-for-One looked at him and told him that she was new. And the prettiest social worker that came through here.

Two-for-One had all of the necessities to live in prison. He told Darell, "You can use some of my deodorant and stuff, but don't act like it's yours." Now that he knew Darell wasn't lying about his crime, he felt a little comfortable with him. Since he stole a cop's car, he knew Darell wasn't too pleased with any officers. "Maybe he's just a rebel or a spoiled brat," he said to himself.

"Try to get a job in here or a hustle. Working in the kitchen or in the infirmary is the best jobs around here. You get to see a lot of women."

"Do they be fighting a lot in here?"

"Every now and then. But in this unit we get a lot of cell gangsters. You got to remember one thing in prison," Two-for-One said as he walked over to the cell door and peeped out, "Ain't nobody tough in prison. Anybody could get hit. I'm getting ready to get this shank from this officer's desk. And when I do, they're going to lock down this whole unit to search for it."

Two-for-One waited for the hospital porter to bring him a piece of chewing gum that was thrown away by a female corrections officer. Her gum chewing annoyed all of the inmates in his unit and in the infirmary so much, that they complained to the superintendent. She was so good at popping gum, she could pop gum ten times in one second. At times she would rapidly pop for thirty seconds.

Inmates weren't able to sleep as she popped. Their complaints to the supervisor were useless. So each day about twenty letters were sent to the commissioner's office from the inmates. The commissioner ordered the superintendent at the reception facility to personally investigate the situation. When he went to investigate it, he walked off of the elevator and the rapid sound of gum popping echoed off the walls. It was loud but not irritating to him. But to try and sleep with that sound was impossible. He didn't bother to walk down to the officer. He just looked down the infirmary, waved at the officers down there, and got back on the elevator.

The next day he had a memo out banning all gum chewing for all staff members. After that, there were no more complaints. Two-for-One received his last piece of gum, and decided to get his weapon. He waited for the officer to walk down the tier to grab the Lexan plastic clipboard off the officer's desk. The board was one of the chief's pet peeves. This was his masterpiece. This plastic clipboard replaced the housing unit officer's wooden clipboard. The chief decided to buy plastic clipboards for all the units. That was the greatest discovery that he came up with at the reception unit. This clipboard was also a good weapon for the inmates. Two-for-One took the clipboard off of the desk and broke the top part off of it. That part had the metal clamp on it. He explained to the rookie officer, how he accidentally knocked it off the desk, as he was wiping off the desk and the clipboard fell on the floor. He showed the officer the top broken half and threw it in the trash can. He told the rookie officer that the regular officer would get another clipboard from the storeroom, making it seem like they break clipboards every week in that unit.

After the officer agreed to that, he took all of the trash out to the trash bins. While at the bin, he took the broken piece out, tucked it in his socks and carried it to his cell. That afternoon during outside recreation, he took a small rock from the ground in the yard, and sharpened the edge of the metal piece in his cell. He put tape on the non-sharpened end to make the handle.

To hide the shank, he soaked the five pieces of gum that he had in hot water. An hour later he rechewed the gum. The gum was then placed on one side of the shank, and placed firmly underneath the top of the officer's desk. He knew that the last place the officers would search was the officer's desk. Two days later, after the rookie officer was questioned, the tier was locked down and searched. The broken piece was never found and the lock down ended.

"See, you always have to think like an officer. Always think about where an inmate will hide his stash, not where he won't hide it at," he told Darell. "If you need to use it for fighting, you know where it's at." Darell smiled at him as Two-for-One left the cell.

Later that day, the assistant superintendent toured the unit with the chief of corrections escorting her. Darell was astonished by her beauty and her fashionable African style of clothes. She looked like a queen, and smelled as if she was wearing the finest of perfume oils. Her high heel shoes allowed her height to be six feet two inches. She knew after shake downs and cell searches, come the inmate complaints. The complaints from inmates always came to her. The tour of the unit prepared her to be one step ahead of all of the paperwork she'd be getting. The chief that was with her, was criticized and reprimanded by her for putting those kind of clipboards on the units. He refused to believe that the broken pieces were thrown away. He knew it could be made into a good weapon by an inmate. The only inmate that could have taken it was Two-for-One, he thought. And for him to be in number one cell, the cell that's the closest to the officer's desk, Two-for-One had easy access to it.

After the chief entered the unit with the assistant superintendent, he ordered the officer to pat search Darell and Two-for-One. They walked out of their cell to be patted down. Darell walked out with an empty eight-ounce Styrofoam cup in his hand.

"That piece has to be in here somewhere. I know it has to be," the chief told the superintendent.

"Hey! Pull your jumper up. Don't let your jumper sag off your waist like that." Darell wrapped the top part of his jumper around and below his waist as he walked out of his cell. He was used to letting his pants sag off of his waist when he was on the streets. That's just the way the younger generation did it in the neighborhood. That was the way he walked on the streets in the hood. After the officer pat searched Darell, Darell walked over to the water fountain to pour water in his cup. The chief continued, "You're not on the street. You will wear that jumper the right way when you come out of that cell. Didn't your father teach you how to dress?"

The chief looked at the officer and said, "His pop probably sag his pants, too. He probably have a young father too, huh."

Darell looked like a young adolescent to the chief. The chief thought he probably was charged as an adult. While pouring water into the cup, Darell reflected on his father's words on clothes, especially a man's shoes. And he did not appreciate the chief talking about his father.

"You need to set an example for all of the other new inmates that come in here. Don't pull your pants down like that no more, inmate." Darell noticed the chief's dull and dirty shoes, and asked him, as he held the cup of water in his hand, "Do you set the example for the officers to follow by the way you dress?"

The chief walked over to Darell at the water fountain and said, "Yes, I set a fine example for my officers, if you must know."

Darell looked down at the chief's shoes as the chief stood in front of him and said, "What about your shoes?"

"What about my shoes?" he asked Darell.

Darell poured the water from his cup onto the chief's shoes, and at the same time told him, "They're dirty. You need to clean them."

The chief called the sergeant and the lieutenant by radio. The officer told Darell to put his hands on the wall and face it. He was handcuffed and escorted off of the unit to a lockup unit. Although the chief was embarrassed, he knew Darell was right. But to be embarrassed and insulted in front of the superintendent made him more furious.

While in lockup, Darell was escorted from there to the psychologist's office to complete his evaluation. Darell was charged with assault. His mental status had to be determined first, to rule if he is guilty or not. The same psychologist who questioned him earlier, questioned him again.

"Young man," the psychologist said as he looked at Darell with a worried look, "Is there something troubling you? Is there something bothering you? Or you just don't like to be in prison." Darell left this man's office earlier with the thought of not returning for about a week later. Now he had to listen to more of the annoying questions.

"Darell, could it be that maybe you're the problem?"

Darell sat in the chair handcuffed, refusing to talk.

"Pretend that I'm not a psychologist. Act like I'm a judge. Tell me why you decided to pour water on the chief's shoes."

Darell chuckled a little, and looked down at the psychologist's dull and dirty shoes and explained the assault.

"My father is dead. The chief insulted my father, by in so many words, saying that my father didn't know how to dress. My father was one of the best dressed men in Trenton. He told me before he died, to keep my shoes shined. The chief told me that he represented the officers in the way he dressed. In which was a lie because his shoes were dusty and dirty. And the first responsibility of a man and his shoes is to wax and shine them. Even if the pants and shirt isn't clean, the shoes is what counts."

The psychologist determined that Darell wasn't crazy, but mad at the way his father was insulted. After he completed the evaluation, Darell was escorted back to the lockup unit, and waited for the hearing. The next day, an inmate paralegal, named Cook, was assigned to represent him. Cook was the only inmate or probably the only person throughout the inmate population, who believed that a person was innocent until proven guilty.

After Cook read Darell's charge sheet, and what the chief wrote, Cook told Darell what really happened in his opinion.

"What happened was. It was an accident. You feel me. See, you filled the cup up with too much water, and the water spilled out as you walked by the chief," Cook told Darell, as he talked to him through the cell bars. Cook's concept of a charge, that an officer writes on an inmate, is that it's just the officers opinion of what happened. The judge is the one who determines the case.

"Cause if you really wanted to throw water on him, you could've threw it in his face. He said you poured water on his shoes. That's a lie. He just wanted to impress the superintendent lady, that's all."

Cook read the charge sheet again, nodded his head and said, "We can beat this charge." Darell smiled at him and started to laugh. He was impressed at Cook's synopsis of the event. For a few seconds Darell believed that's what really happened, too.

"You're good. You're real good," he said to Cook as he continued laughing.

Out of all of the accusations and charges Darell was accused of, nobody sided with him. Everybody just wanted him to plead guilty and make plea bargains. Cook was the first to try and back him up.

"I appreciate you trying to look out for me. But I did pour water on his shoes. The man talked about my pop. So I talked about his shoes and told him to clean them."

Cook never had an inmate he defended plead guilty on him. He thought Darell was young and mentally distraught.

"Maybe we can talk to the psychologist and have him say you're mentally challenged or something."

"I already talked to the psychologist. I told him to shine his shoes, too."

Cook looked at his state issued boots to make sure they weren't dirty.

"Well, you won't be telling me to clean my shoes. My wears are always tight. But listen," Cook told him as he moved closer to the bars. "You should plead guilty with an explanation. Then you can tell them why you did it". Cook saw that Darell didn't regret the assault and was determined to tell the truth about it. He knew that Darell was new at this and didn't know the consequences of it. If found guilty of assault at this reception facility, he would be transferred to Trenton State Prison. Assaults and fights occur regularly at Trenton State. The prison houses maximum security inmates. The majority of the state's murderers are there.

He didn't want to tell him that, because he didn't want to scare him. So he thought about asking for leniency with the guilty plea. With Darell's baby face and timid look, he knew Darell wasn't going to last at Trenton State without another inmate trying to make him his girl. While Cook was working on Darell's defense at the same time the chief who was assaulted by Darell was pressuring the hearing officer to find him guilty.

"These kids have no respect for anything or anybody. We need to show them an example when they attack us. I think he's one of those gang bangers," the chief said to the hearing officer while sitting in her office. "He's probably with the Bloods or Creeps or whatever you call them. I don't like his attitude or the way he looks." The hearing officer looked in Darell's folder, saw his picture and noticed his age.

"He looks like he's twelve years old," she said. "Maybe he wanted you to look neat like his father or something," She looked down at the chief's shoes and said jokingly as she grabbed her bottled water, "So you want some more water for your shoes? They do look kind of dirty".

He didn't find that funny. He continued talking to her to convince her to find Darell guilty.

"I haven't written an inmate charge in ten years. And you know that I don't bother nobody. I just was walking with the assistant superintendent, minding my business. When I asked that kid to pull his jumper up, he got an attitude with me."

The following day was judgment day for Darell. His hearing was inside of the reception facility at the lockup unit. He was expecting to take a ride to a state or county courthouse, the usual visit for those charged with crimes. The paralegal Cook was there, ready to defend him. But as Darell looked at the woman who was to determine his innocence, he felt confident in what he was about to say. He really didn't need Cook.

The court hearing officer was to determine his guilt or innocence. She was a young woman, with a pretty face and a pleasant voice. The kind of woman he knew would understand the importance of a man's shoes. She was fashionably dressed in civilian clothes. The Court Hearing Officer was a female corrections officer with a cute face, and silky hair. Darell glanced at her pretty white teeth as she smiled and then he stared at her figure.

His question to himself was why would a cute woman like this want to be in this negative environment working as an officer. She looked at him as he stood at the cell bars waiting to be heard next. When their eyes met, he thought about all of the jazz clubs in Philadelphia he would take her to in his Benz. Darell was wondering if she was feeling him, too.

"Maybe I'll see her on the blocks," he thought.

The hearing officer called Darell up to the gate to hear his case.

"Steps, you're charged with assaulting a person," she told him. "How do you plead? Guilty or not guilty?" Cook looked at him, and nodded his head and said, "Handle your business."

"I'm pleading guilty with an explanation."

"So, Mr. Steps, you're pleading guilty?"

"No, I'm pleading guilty with an explanation."

The hearing officer leaned back in her chair, folded her hands, and placed them on her stomach. She realized what the chief said must have been true.

"Okay, Mr. Steps. Explain the assault."

As he began to talk about the incident, she began to write on the back of the charge sheet. He went on talking about men, women, shoes, and how a lady should be treated. She agreed with what he was saying by occasionally saying, "Uh-huh." The female corrections officer smiled at him, as he talked about men who are supposed to set the example. He continued to put his mack down, feeling good as he tried to talk his way out of a guilty plea. When he finished talking the two women were impressed at what he said. The hearing officer smiled and asked him,

"Is there anything else, Mr. Steps?"

"No. That's basically it."

After the ladies briefly looked at each other, the hearing officer turned toward Darell. "Mr. Steps, I find you guilty as charged. I'm ordering you three days locked up. With credit time served. Thirty days lost of commutation time. And refer you to classification." She gave him papers to appeal her decision and said, "You can appeal my decision if you want."

Darell didn't understand anything she said. All he knew was that he pleaded guilty and she agreed with him. He spent three days in lockup. So that was the credit time served. Today was his last day and tomorrow he'll be free. He was elated to know that his mack skills were tight. So he thanked her for giving him the opportunity to explain himself. And he wished both of the women a very nice day.

Darell's appeal to the assistant superintendent was rejected that same day. It was rejected by the same assistant superintendent that was with the chief who Darell assaulted. The early morning wake up call Darell received made him feel like a new man. They told him to pack up, but didn't tell him where he was going. He was escorted off the tier to be transferred to Trenton State Prison.

While being escorted to another holding area, the officer that was with him said, "I hope you're fight skills are tight."

Darell glanced at him and said, "I'm good at what I do."

"That's good," the officer said as they continued to walk.

"You're going to Trenton State Prison. I hope you make some new friends real fast. You're going to need somebody to look out for you when you get there."

Darell stopped walking, and stared at the officer's eyes to see if he was lying.

"That's what happens when you assault an officer."

Darell hesitated to move, and looked worried.

"What? You need my gun? You scared or something? Ain't you from out Wilbur section in Trenton?"

Somehow, the thought of the streets gave Darell the courage to walk again. Out of all of the war stories he's heard about Trenton State Prison, he'll be there to witness them.

"Bubba needs a new cell mate," the officer said laughing. "He needs somebody to wash his underwear."

"I ain't scared of no Bubba. I might have him washing my clothes for me. And if you call him before I get there, tell him he better not be laying in my bed either."

They walked and talked the rest of the way to the admission and discharge area. The wait for the transfer to Trenton State Prison was long. As he waited, Darell slept face down on the holding cell bench. The psychologist who interviewed him noticed Darell laying there sleeping. After picking up some folders, he walked into the holding cell where Darell was laying. Darell faintly heard foot steps coming toward him. Those foot steps stopped at his head. While laying face down, he opened his eyes and saw a pair of shiny black shoes. The black pants were wrinkled too. He looked up and saw that same familiar looking psychologist smiling at him. Feeling constructively criticized, he took Darell's advice and shined his shoes, in hopes to represent the real men in society.

"Take care and stay out of trouble," he told Darell. After shaking Darell's hand, he left the area.

CHAPTER 4

The ride to Trenton State Prison took him to the outskirts of Trenton. The familiar sights brought back memories to him. While riding to the state prison, he noticed the Delaware River that was to his right. As he rode past the low and dirty river, Darell thought about how he used to fish and swim in that river. The south side of Trenton was the part of Trenton he tried to avoid. This side of Trenton was where the prison was at. And now, he had to live in the south side of Trenton for ten years. The thought of him living among the state's most notorious prisoners made him nervous. Father Time's words to him encourage him as he reflected back on them.

"Everything that's inside of the prison came from the outside. If you're not afraid of what's outside here, then don't be afraid of what's in there."

After he entered the prison, one of the officers told him, "We heard about your assault charge. We usually spank inmates who assault officers, as an initiation, when they get here. But nobody likes that chief. Don't get used to hitting officers here. This is, your only warning."

Darell went through the normal routine of stripping and being searched. All transferred inmates were in the intake area. As he looked around this area, he noticed that all eyes were on him.

"I ain't trying to be nobody's woman in here," he said to himself. Darell noticed a tall six foot six inch man with upper arms as big as him, with an ugly face. He wondered if this was Bubba. He couldn't figure out the words that were written on his upper right arm, but the image of him was intimidating. This inmate's nickname was Tomahawk. He worked in this intake area, processing the paperwork for all prisoners that were coming to, and leaving this prison. Throughout the prison, he had a gruesome and brutal reputation. But Tomahawk was not a bully and didn't talk to many inmates.

As Darell sat waiting, another inmate who was known on the street as Muscleman the Hustleman, noticed Darell. Half of the appliances in Darell's mom's house were bought from him. The last purchase his mother bought from Muscleman was Darell's stereo. She still owed Muscleman money for it, but he got locked up and never got paid. Muscleman worked in the intake area also. It was his second year in prison and his second year working in this area of the prison. As he walked towards Darell smiling, he said to him, "What's up, Dew Drop?" That was what Muscleman called Darell on the street, because of his size.

"I'm surprised to see you here." He shook Darell's hand and gave him a half hug. He took a step back and looked at Darell. "The police ain't raided your house and confiscated your stereo, did they?"

"Naw, but the police said he was going to move in my room when I'm gone. I think he's big on my mom."

"Oh. I thought they locked you up for having my goods. But you know that all of my sells are legitimate, right?"

"Don't play yourself, Hustleman. Your name's not even legit. The only reason why ain't nobody told on you out there is because they don't know your real name."

"Well they knew me enough to describe me. But I am a respectable businessman."

"You crazy!"

"For real. Ask your mom. She'll tell you. Hey! Your mom still owes me two hundred dollars. I ain't forget."

"She had the money. You just didn't come by to pick it up."

"I was coming by, but I got picked up." They laughed as Muscleman explained. "They said that I violated my parole when I left the state. Now I'm here for another year and all of this will be over. Hey! You need anything? I got connections. I can get you what you want in here."

"Anything? Like what?" Darell asked hoping he could get a pass home.

"Do you need smokes? Protection? A used radio for your cell? What do you need? I'll get it. You know how I do. You might need some protection from these inmates, unless your fight skills are tight. This place ain't no joke."

"Okay. Get me a nine gun, with hollow point bullets."

"Fool! Ain't nobody bringing no gun in prison. If they did, I would have one. I can get you a nice size shank, though."

"I know you're good at getting TVs and radios. And now you're selling shanks too, huh?"

"My man, Snake, selling all the weapons. I'm just the middleman. You know the go-between man."

"I don't want a nice size shank. I want one that's going to get the job done."

"Listen." Muscleman told him as he looked around from side to side.

"I can get you a sword if you want one, Dew Drop."

"Stop playing. Ain't nobody bringing no swords in prison."

"Naw. Naw. Snake got one on top of his cell. He ain't used it on nobody either. It's right on top of his cell, too." He thought about a price and told Darell, "It'll cost you about a hundred packs of cigarettes."

"I ain't got no smokes, Muscleman. You know that."

"Well, that's how we do here. So if you need it holla at me. And holla at your mom and tell her to put my two hundred dollars in my account here. I can use that for something." Hustleman paused as his jailhouse and street friend Leroy was walking towards the exit door. Leroy had just finished serving nineteen years in prison for armed robbery and other petty crimes. Leroy is the new administrator's (Mr. Graves), older of four brothers. As he wrote his brother from prison, Leroy's letters to his brother always stressed the importance about staying in school and staying off the streets. It is known throughout their neighborhood in the Wilbur section of Trenton, that all of his brothers have a fast temper and a low tolerance in any disagreement. Violence was their way of life. This is Leroy's last day in prison, and he's about to be released from this intake area. For nineteen years, he survived the brutality, and challenges in prison. Now his life will continue once again, on the streets.

"Hey Lee!"

Braking up a persons name regardless of how it's really pronounced was Muscleman's way of life.

"I'll get with you later Dew Drop. I gotta holla at my people over there before they leave."

After shaking hands, Darell was called by the nurse. She gave him a small bottle for his urine sample. Darell waited to be the last one to go to the restroom with the other new prisoners. Some of them had double life sentences to do, and will never be on the streets again. And they didn't care about who they hurt while they were in prison, because prison was their home for life; they were never leaving prison. Giving them more time was useless. All of them were much older, and bigger than he was. Some of the men didn't look at Darell's size as short and skinny. They looked at his size as petite. Darell went into the restroom after everyone exited it and was told by the officer, not to be long in there. He went into the toilet stall and closed the door. One minute later as he was about to leave the stall, someone else came into the restroom and walked pass the stall Darell was in.

Darell decided to stay in the toilet area out of sight with the door closed. Not knowing if that man who walked in, was one of those men that was looking at him in the shower, that was on the down low and liked little boys. A second man entered the restroom and walked straight to the sink to wash his hands in front of the toilet stall Darell was in.

Darell peeped out of the slit in the door where the door latch was and saw an axe tattoo on the man's upper arm. Above the axe was the word Tomahawk. This inmate, Tomahawk, began to question the first inmate that came into the restroom.

"Hey! You just got here, huh? I know you from Trenton. I seen you on the blocks out there somewhere." Tomahawk talked to the man as if they were friends. The man walked over to the sink to wash his hands next to Tomahawk. Tomahawk continued to talk to the man, "Do you know Jimmy Keys?"

"That name sounds familiar. I might know him if I see him," the inmate said as he tried to picture Jimmy Keys face.

"You won't see him anymore," Tomahawk told him as he punched the man in his face knocking the man down.

"That was my ten-year-old son you raped and killed." Tomahawk pulled out a Plexiglas shank and stabbed him in the chest. Half of the weapon had broken off and was embedded in the man's chest when he stabbed him. And the other half Tomahawk threw in the garbage can in front of the toilet stall.

After Tomahawk left, Darell walked out of the toilet area and saw the man lying on his back, with half of the weapon sticking out of his chest. Darell saw that he wasn't moving, that's when he panicked and ran to the door and peeped out. He saw Tomahawk talking to a correction officer, shaking his head as if he was saying no. The officer started to walk in Darell's direction knowing that he sent Darell to the restroom. Darell closed the door and began to sweat, looking for another way out. Not seeing another way out, he thought about what to do. He didn't want to tell on Tomahawk. That would have made him a rat. Father Time told him about what other inmates do to snitches in prison. And it wasn't anything nice.

Since this man was a child rapist, Darell decided to take the blame for this. Darell thought he had a better chance saying he killed the man in self defense, because the man tried to rape him. He heard Tomahawk say this man raped his son. So this would save Tomahawk from doing more time for revenge, and he wouldn't be known as a snitch. Plus, this would be one less boy rapist Darell would have to worry about while he's taking a shower. Darell ran to the garbage can, took the broken weapon out and wiped the blood and finger prints on his pants.

He ran back to the door, casually walked out and met the officer as he exited.

"I told you not to be long in there. See you're hardheaded. Is anybody else in there?" Darell looked back at the restroom door and told him,

"Yeah, there's another man in there." He handed the officer the bag of specimen with his left hand and told him about the weapon.

"Here's my specimen, and here's a piece of my shank. The other half is sticking out of the man's chest. He's on the floor. I got to go. Have a nice day."

The officer took the piece of weapon and stared at Darell to see if he was crazy. As Darell walked away the officer hollered, "Hold . . . hold . . . hold it! Come here. Come here." He walked over to Darell and grabbed him by his shirt. The other officer sitting at the desk saw the commotion and stood up. The sergeant in the area saw the officer stand up, but didn't know what was going on.

The officer holding Darell opened the restroom door and saw the inmate lying on the floor with just his legs in view.

"Sarg!" he called out as he pulled Darell by his shirt into the restroom.

The sergeant stood up as the other officer ran toward the restroom. By this time, Tomahawk had left the area, and was on his way to his housing unit. He saw the inmate paralegal who was known throughout the prison as Law. Law had been Tomahawk's confidant for fifteen years in prison. Law was sentenced to ninety-nine years plus three life sentences. He knew he was never leaving prison. He'd been taking criminal justice college courses for over fifteen years in prison. Inmate Law constantly studied the Bible, the Koran and Jewish theology. He also studied psychiatry and sociology and had a PhD in both of them while in prison.

Some inmates felt that he was so good interpreting the law, that if Satan were his client, he would have him found not guilty for all of his crimes against humanity. Law believed in, you get what you pay for; whereas if inmates do not pay him for his services, they usually lose their case. The administration sometimes used his service whenever there seemed to be a no-win situation against the inmates. If there was a class action lawsuit against the administrator, he used Law, for a fee, for counseling. Law gave the perspective from both sides of the law. That's because he knew both sides of the law.

Tomahawk hired Law to represent him for the premeditated murder. They had discussed the incident the day before when Tomahawk told him his son's killer was scheduled to come to Trenton State Prison. Law told him not to kill him because Tomahawk had a good chance of being paroled within a year. Tomahawk told him that he couldn't be living on the streets peacefully knowing that he met his son's killer in prison and didn't get revenge.

After leaving the intake area, Tomahawk saw inmate Law and was walking toward him to tell him what happened when they heard an announcement of Codes on the intercom.

"Code 50" (Emergency medical attention)

"Code 30" (Custody emergency response)

"Code 20" (Lock down stand up count)

No words were spoken between the two, so Law only assumed that Tomahawk killed the man. They stopped and stared at each other, and walked away. Darell was placed in lockup status. The prison was locked down. All inmates were confined to their cells all day. Once again, murder charges were brought against Darell.

Tomahawk packed up everything in his cell, and stood at his cell door waiting for the officers to escort him to the detention area of the prison. This is the prison's lock-up area. Finally, at six thirty in the morning, breakfast came through. He had been up all night standing, sitting, walking, and worrying, during the lock down. His anticipated escort never showed up. Therefore, he ate breakfast and went to sleep.

Law ate breakfast and was told by an officer to get dressed, because he had to go and defend a murderer.

"Tomahawk saw the transfer papers. He knew who was coming in. He knew the man raped his son. So it was premeditated," Law stated to himself. "The man tried to rape Tomahawk. Yeah, that might work. No. No. No. That doesn't even sound right." Law contemplated about Tomahawk's defense as he washed his face. "We're just gonna have to make a deal and plea for leniency."

During the lock down, Law was escorted over to the west side of the prison by an officer. The officers who work in that unit had no love for Law. Law always found ways to get an inmate found not guilty, and make it seem that all of the officers had personal problems. Therefore, he lied on every officer that wrote a charge on an inmate. He was wondering if the response team beat Tomahawk when they took him from his housing unit. Law greeted the lockup unit officers as he entered the unit.

"Good Morning, Officers. How are y'all doing today? It is such a lovely day this morning. Don't you think so?" Law said this to the officers as they patted him down.

"Go to number fifty-two cell and talk to your client. I don't want to talk," the officer responded. "And when you finish with him I have somebody else for you to defend."

Law walked up to Darell's cell, number fifty-two, looking for Tomahawk. Darell looked at him as Law stood at his door. Law took a step back and looked at the door number again. He thought,

"Maybe they want me to talk to Tomahawk last. His charge is more serious." He looked at Darell again and thought he was a juvenile about fourteen years old.

"What's up, yo? How you?" Darell nodded his head as he sat up on his bed.

"I'm your paralegal. They call me Law."

"I'm Darell Steps. From Wilbur section in Trenton. I ain't trying to make no deals and plea bargain with these people either."

Law had no paperwork on him. The officers did not give him any when they were supposed to and he did not ask for any. All he wanted to do was to talk to Tomahawk.

"How much time you doing here?" Law asked him.

"What time is it now?"

"Nine o'clock."

"I'm doing about twenty-four. I just got here yesterday."

"You doing twenty-four years?" Law asked jokingly, thinking that this youngster was on the streets gang banging. "What? You done shot up somebody and couldn't get a deal? What you done did now?"

Darell responded to him with an attitude, "I just got here yesterday, fool. I told you I've been here twenty-four hours, fool. Not twenty-four years. What are you, stupid or something? Can you tell time?" Darell was getting louder and louder as he talked.

"Add up from yesterday until now. How much time is that, fool?"

He stood up from his bed and walked over to Law.

Law told Darell, "You better lower your voice when you talk to me. I ain't your problem."

Darell over talked him. "You is my problem, you idiot. They sent this idiot to my cell." He hollered out loud to the officers, "Hey! Officers! Get this idiot away from my cell door!"

Law hollered down to the officers, too. "Bust number fifty-two cell. And let's see how much gangster he got in him when his cell door is open."

One officer approached the scene and asked them what all the shouting was for.

Darell told Law as the officer came to his cell, “You’ll get your feelings hurt if you come up in my cell, punk.”

The officer told Law to go back down stairs to see his other client.

“No!” Law told him. “Open his door. He sounds like a tough guy. Open his door.”

The other officer came up there, threatened to kick him out of the area and get another paralegal. Law walked off the tier fuming.

“These young boys just don’t know. I ain’t no joke. That boy acted as if he wants some work with his hands. This ain’t no juvenile detention center,” Law stated as he walked down the stairs.

“I’m ma see him when he get out. I swear on my mom, I’m ma get with him when he gets out.” He walked to the officer’s desk shaking his head, feeling vexed and walking around in circles. “I don’t know why y’all sent me to him. See y’all got game with y’all. I don’t have time for this. This ain’t what I came over here for. Y’all try to set me up.”

Law looked on the officer’s desk for Tomahawk’s cell number. “Where’s Tomahawk’s cell? That’s who I come here to see anyway.”

The officers look at Law and one of them told him, “Tomahawk ain’t over here. Here are copies of that boy’s charge and this inmate in number ten cells needs to talk to you.”

“Where did they take Tomahawk?”

“I told you Tomahawk’s not over here. Are you gonna see this inmate or not?”

“Yeah. I’ll see him. But I’m supposed to defend somebody for that murder yesterday, ain’t I.”

Thinking that the officers banged Tomahawk up and sent him to the hospital, he asked, “Did they take Tomahawk to the hospital?”

One of the officers was annoyed with the Tomahawk question and asked him as he stood up, "What do Tomahawk got to do with this?" He was angry and ready to throw him out of the lockup area.

Law answered the officers as if they knew that Tomahawk murdered the inmate, but now were acting stupid.

"Didn't Tomahawk stab that inmate yesterday?"

He waited for the answer to prove him right.

"No. Tomahawk ain't stabbed nobody. Unless you know something we don't know." Both officers looked at Law and waited for a response. One of the officers asked Law, "Do you feel like talking?"

Law looked dumbfounded and asked, "Who stabbed that inmate yesterday?"

"That boy you just argued with," one of the officers told him. "I just gave you the copy of that boy's charges."

Law began to read Darell's charges. He was shocked and confused by what he was reading. As he read on, he slowly walked over to the officer's chair and sat in it.

"You better find you another seat and get up out of mine. There's no cell bars between us, and I ain't gonna argue with you."

Law quickly stood up and walked over to the wall, facing it. After reading the charge sheet, he held it down to his legs and began talking facing the wall. His back was toward the officers, but they heard him as he talked.

"They railroaded this boy. They railroaded him. I know it. They told him to say this. They told him to say he stabbed the man. They couldn't find the real killer, so they picked one. Yeah, that's what they did." He began to laugh, still facing the wall.

"This boy don't know no better. They ran a game on him. That's what they did." Law started laughing harder, knowing that the administration didn't know who the killer is.

The officers were thinking that Law might be going crazy. "I think them fifteen years starting to get to you. I can't imagine how you'll be acting when you do those three hundred years." Both officers burst out laughing at Law, thinking that he was going crazy. They did not realize what Law was laughing about.

When the laughter ended, Law faced reality. To Law, Darell was the scapegoat. Maybe the administration wanted the word to get out that Darell was the killer, so if someone else talked and bragged about how he killed the inmate, they could use that against him. There is no statute of limitation for murder. Tomahawk was up for parole within a year. In addition, the administration needed concrete evidence for a conviction.

However, waiting another year to find out the truth was not happening for Law. He wanted to stay on top of it. He thought Darell was someone that was just randomly picked out of the crowd and was coerced to confess to the murder. However, what he did not know was that Darell was just the witness to the murder.

Law developed no love of words with Darell, after his one and only visit with him. He was elated that his boy Tomahawk was not charged, but he also was cautious. He needed to approach Darell, but in a different way. The officers allowed him to talk to Darell again. He stood in front of his cell door as Darell lay on his bed with both his hands behind his head, looking up at the ceiling.

Law did not know if he should have apologized first, or just start talking about the charge. When Darell saw him at his cell door, he gave him a warning,

"Don't let this pretty face fool you. I hit hard."

"I don't want no trouble. I come in peace." Law showed him a copy of the charge sheet and said to him, "I read this copy of your charge sheet." Darell looked at the paper Law was holding.

"So. I read the sheet, too."

"You could beat this. There are no self-defense laws in New Jersey, but I can see this man attacking you. And you ain't no punk, so you did what you had to do. You're probably not the first person he attacked, and you wasn't going to wait to find out.

Any jury could see that. They assigned me to this case, and that's how I see it."

Darell looked back up at the ceiling and told him, "It's nice to hear that you're not talking like an idiot. And, that's how I see it too."

Law is wondering if this is how Darell really saw it, or if this is what really happened. Darell felt a little more comfortable because Law did not come to him talking about making a deal. Plea bargaining could not be in the conversation with Darell. He needed somebody to defend him that thought the way he did.

"Now go represent and tell the administration what you just told me, too."

"Alright. I'll holla at you tomorrow. Im'ma type this up right now." As he turned to walk away from the cell, Darell called him. Darell decided to take the officers advice from the reception facility, and make a new friend quick at this prison. What better friend to have than one of the most fearsome inmates in this prison.

"Hey. Do you know Tomahawk, Yo?"

Without thinking Law responded, "Yeah. That's my dog. You know my dog, huh?"

"Yeah, I know Tomahawk."

Law thought Darell had heard about Tomahawk while he was at the county jail. "How do you know Tomahawk?"

Darell sat up and sat on the edge of the bed and said, "That's my father." Those words shocked Law. His mouth opened up and froze in that position.

"If you see him, tell him that Snake sells good shanks, and they don't break either."

Law remembered reading about a broken off piece of plastic given to the officer, but why was it mentioned, and why deliver that message to Tomahawk.

Law hasn't talked to Tomahawk since the murder incident happened. Now he knew why Tomahawk was not locked up. **He had his son kill the man**. He knew his son was coming to prison, and Tomahawk was scheduled to leave next year. This way he would not be charged for it, and do any more time for the murder.

"That was real smooth," he said about Tomahawk.

"I got to get his son off of this murder charge."

As he was escorted from the lockup area, Law remembered talking with Tomahawk about his son's death. He stopped walking with the officer, and then said to himself, "He never told me he had another son."

That thought was on his mind as the officer escorted him back to his housing unit. And it stayed on his mind until the lock down ended.

CHAPTER 5

The administrator determined that the attack was not gang related and that it was an isolated incident. The next day, the prison lock down was partially lifted. Mess movements, hospital passes, and paralegals were the only ones allowed to move in the prison.

Law walked to the mess hall looking for Tomahawk. Tomahawk refused to leave his cell, thinking that the officer would raid his cell. While thinking about it, he opened boxes and flushed down the toilet all news clippings of his son's death. These clippings had his son's killer name in them, too. The feeling of anxiety forced Law to walk over to Tomahawk's housing unit to talk to him, to let him know that he met his prodigy. The fake paralegal work for the inmates in the housing unit got him through the gate and was told by the officer, that Tomahawk was in the shower. He turned and saw a massive body walking from the shower toward him. Law met him halfway as they walked toward each other.

They shook hands, half hugged, and began to talk to each other.

"They ain't been over here yet looking for me. I hooked off on him with a right hand and dropped him. Officer King saw me coming out of the toilet area. What is he saying about me?"

Now Law felt like he was being played, feeling deceived. Now he's thinking, maybe the officer had the real story to this. Maybe it was a family thing; whereas Tomahawk and his son stabbed the man, and the son got caught.

"What is he supposed to say about you?"

"About him, seeing me, coming out of the restroom. Is he talking about him seeing me? He asked me if anybody else was in the restroom when I left. I told him no. He was on his way in there. He knew I lied to him. Or maybe he's just not talking."

"Somebody else already talked and told," Law told him, hoping that he will mention his son.

"Who? The sergeant? He was over there. Did the sergeant say something? Who talked?"

Law stepped closer to Tomahawk, pointing at him as he talked, to let him know that he knew about Tomahawk's son.

"This eighteen-year-old boy told Officer King, he stabbed the inmate and broke a piece of shank off in him."

Tomahawk thought he was lying. "There wasn't nobody else in there. You're lying."

"I read the charge sheet, and saw the picture of the weapon."

Law backed up a little to think to himself, putting his thumb and finger on his chin.

"Did you look in the toilet stall? Was the toilet stall door open? You think somebody else came in and saw you as your back was turned and walked out?"

"Listen, if somebody else was in there, or came in and left, why would they claim a body like that, Law?"

"I don't know, but that's not the shocker."

"That is the shocker," Tomahawk snapped back.

"But if he wants to be responsible for the body, then let him have it."

Law stood in front of him with his head down shaking it from side to side. What was supposed to be a simple murder has now become so complicated. He is either protecting his son, or did not know his son. The son has to be discussed. Looking in his eyes, Law asked, "Do you know Darell Steps?"

"I can't remember if I do. Does he know me?"

"He says he does."

With a confused look on his face, Tomahawk asked, "So is that the shocker?"

"The shocker is that, this boy is saying you're his father. That's the shocker".

Tomahawk is speechless, knowing that his one and only son was murdered.

"That boy's lying. How old you said he was? Eighteen? Naw. That ain't my son. He's lying."

They started to add up their time in prison and their arrests. Both were arrested in the same month, in the same year, nineteen years ago. Tomahawk became confused with the date and asked, "Well, what's his mom's name."

"I didn't ask him all that. Who was the last woman you been with, when you was out there on the streets."

Tomahawk forgot that the last woman he spent time with was Law's wife.

"Uh, Darlene what's her name. Darlene Cook. That might be his mom."

"Darlene Cook", Law shouted back. "You got my ex-wife pregnant? You been creeping with my wife?"

"Naw. Naw. Not Darlene. Her friend Darlene. The one that lives in Hamilton Township. You know, dark-skinned Darlene. Stop playing, Law."

"Let me find out you been creeping with my wife. She told me I was not the baby's father. That's why I left her."

After a short pause, Law told him, "This doesn't look right or sound right. I'll find out about the boy's family and try to make some sense out of all of this." As they walked down the tier, Law stopped to give Tomahawk his theory; raising his right hand up to his chest as he talked.

"Look this boy was probably told as he sat in the intake area that the man killed his half brother. Hustleman or somebody down there gave the boy a shank. When the man went inside of the rest room, he shanked him. Or maybe he went in the restroom after you left and shanked the man."

Tomahawk felt insulted and could not believe what he just heard. He felt good that someone else took the blame for the assault. This adopted son of his, who he has no idea of who he might be, had been in his work area. If he asked Law about him, why didn't he talk to Tomahawk when they were in that same intake area? That was the question Tomahawk wanted to ask. He gave his version of the incident again, so that Law would have no doubts. While telling the story, his anger and frustration got the best of him. The more he talked the louder he got.

"I care less about what you heard, or what you been told. I dropped a right hand on him. I shanked him. You gonna let some little punk run game on you? Fine! But don't come to me acting as if I'm crazy or something. Ain't nothing wrong with me. I know what I did. And if anybody else violates me or mine, they'll get gotten, too."

Tomahawk received half of the inmates in that housing unit's attention, including the officer. The officer ordered Law out of the unit and ordered Tomahawk to his cell. After the last lunch mess, rumors circulated through the prison with different versions of the attack. The versions were: Tomahawk's son killed the man. Tomahawk got a hit man to do his dirty work. Tomahawk was recruiting young gang members as soon as they enter the institution, and the initiation to become a member is to kill someone first.

As Darell stood in his cell looking out of the cell window, at a black Benz in the prison parking lot, he heard two officers approaching his cell door. Those officers escorted Darell from lockup, to a large interview room. This room was called the Understanding Room. Internal Affairs officers wanted to question him. The self-defense story was plausible to them. However, they wanted to know where he got the weapon.

Two prep-school-looking Internal Affairs officers were standing in the room waiting for Darell. They were new at this and looked as if they came straight out of the academy. Their strategy was to play the good cop/bad cop position. They preferred that the room be dark with one light in it, with Darell sitting at a small desk. That is the way they visualized it on TV.

The superintendent of the prison, Mr. Graves, walked into the room, took a seat in the corner of the room, and placed a small tape recorder on his lap. He transferred to this prison six months previous from a medium security state prison. The transfer was a personal favor for his best friend, who was the governor of New Jersey. Mr. Graves is known for his stubbornness and his fast temper. Gang members activities are either nonexistent or have a very low profile at Trenton State Prison. Mr. Graves does not tolerate gang activities or gang members. The older inmates at the prison, who are serving endless time, do not care about a gang member either. In addition, those young inmates in there do not know anything about doing time and trying to survive.

"Don't disrespect me and I won't disrespect you" is the word inside.

There is always the hardheaded youth who goes against the odds and learns the hard way. The former goon squad or inmate remedy technician's officers escorted Darell into the interview room. These officers were two of about seven other officers who specialized in riot control and extracting inmates from their cells. One officer named Crusher stood six foot five inches tall, two hundred sixty pounds. His hand was the size of a baseball glove. The other officer that the inmates called Bad News stood at six foot eight, two hundred ninety pounds."

One of these two officers usually escorts the visitors around the institution. The chief of corrections sat in on the interview, too. The Internal Affairs officers introduced themselves to Darell, and began to interrogate. Darell thought they came straight out of a comic book. They repeatedly asked, "Where did you get the weapon?"

Darell repeatedly answered, "I brought it in with me."

They asked a few other questions, but it came back to, "Where did you get the weapon?"

Their strategy was to keep asking and maybe he would break down and tell them.

"We got eight hours to do here. And if you don't talk today, we'll be back tomorrow."

"I got ten years to do here. So I'll be back tomorrow, too," Darell, told them. He knows that to have a reputation as being a rat was not a good way to do ten years in prison. This interview lasted for two hours and forty-five minutes. Mr. Graves saw and heard enough with this interview. He wanted to know where the weapon came from in his prison, and he was not going to wait ten years.

"Uh, excuse me, gentlemen, why don't you take a break. Let me talk to the young man for a minute."

Mr. Graves told the Internal Affairs officers, as he stood up and walked toward Darell.

After the officers left, Mr. Graves sat on the other side of the small table facing Darell. By reading the charge sheet, Mr. Graves notice Darell's age. He also notices Darell's baby face and concluded that Darell was the victim and stabbed the man to protect himself. All Mr. Graves wanted to know was where the weapon came from. The stabbing was justified in his opinion. His question to Darell was very polite and simple. After introducing himself to Darell, Mr. Graves asked him the same question.

"Where did you get the weapon?"

"I told y'all I brought it in with me. That's the same question them other two clowns asked me." Darell turned towards Officer Crusher, and said to the officer about Mr. Graves, "He must not been listening", as he pointed at Mr. Graves.

Mr. Graves grabbed one side of the table and flipped it over, as he stood up.

"I don't have time for this. Lock that door!" he barked at Crusher while taking off his suit jacket. "Bring me that raincoat out of the closet; I don't want to get blood on my clothes."

Darell remained seated as he observed all of the commotion. Mr. Graves continued to give orders. He told the chief, "Give me your belt." The superintendent started rolling up his sleeves as he became angrier. He looked at the officer they called Bad News and ordered him, "Turn that radio on. Turn it up loud."

Crusher gave him the raincoat, and the chief gave him his belt.

"Pick that table up. Crusher!" He shouted, "Take his pants off."

Darell was shocked to hear those words. Not knowing that was what they did in some prisons. He looked at the stain spotted black raincoat as Mr. Graves fastened the buttons up and realized that the stains on the coat were bloodstains. Darell stood up and started walking backwards, looking in all directions. Crusher grabbed him, lifted him up and turned him upside down by his pants. His pants came down to his ankles, and as Crusher pulled them off, the left shoe came off, too.

"You can't call your mom. And Internal Affairs won't hear you." Mr. Graves told him as he wrapped the chief's uniform belt around his hand, leaving the big buckle exposed.

"Put him on the table and hold him down."

Crusher and Bad News grabbed Darell and placed him face down on the table.

"Get off of me. Get off of me," Darell shouted while struggling with the officers. After placing him on the table, Crusher sat down on Darell's back pinning him down. Darell turned his head from side to side, trying to see where Mr. Graves was. When he could not locate him he hollered, "He told me not to tell. He told me not to tell anybody. I ain't wanted to be no rat. He told me not to say nothing."

He continued to struggle, trying to get up and trying to breathe. Mr. Graves walked to the side of him and asked, "Who told you not to tell?"

Mr. Graves saw he was having difficulty breathing. "Let him up Crusher. Let us see what he has to say. Put him in that chair."

The chief asked him, "Who told you not to tell?"

"Snake. He sold me the shank. And he told me not to tell."

"You're lying," Mr. Graves told him.

"Snake's boosting cigarettes and numbers. He isn't selling weapons in my prison. You're lying."

"Yes, he is," Darell, responded as he tried to catch his breath.

"I bought it for ten packs of cigarettes. He wanted to sell me a sword for a hundred packs. I told him no and I got the smaller shank for ten packs."

Mr. Graves stood in front of him with an intimidating look, and ready to swing the belt at him.

"Snake promised me that all of his illegal activities stopped . . . so it's either he's lying or you."

"I think this boy is lying," the chief said. "Snake is up for parole soon. I don't think he'd risk that."

"He told me that those inmates down in intake saw me in the shower, and wanted to talk to me in the restroom. He . . . He . . . He said I'm gonna need something to protect myself. And he said he'll sell me a shank for ten packs."

"So he just walked up to you and sold you a weapon. Just like that?" the chief asked.

"No. I told him I wanted a nine gun with hollow point bullets. He said he couldn't get me that, that he wanted to sell me a sword."

"A sword?" Mr. Graves asked. "Ain't nobody got no sword in here."

"Yes he do. He said he got one right on top of his cell."

Mr. Graves and the chief looked at each other, sensing that Snake lied to them.

"Put your pants on, Boy. Take him back to his cell when he gets dressed."

Darell decided to tell on Snake instead of Hustleman the Muscleman. If Muscleman found out he told on him, Darell's mom might not get any more discounted appliances for the house.

Mr. Graves and the chief remained in the room talking about Snake. Mr. Graves didn't know Snake personally, but knew about his illegal activities. The chief knew Snake's real name, and he also had to battle with Snake in the past. Snake had plenty of institutional charges and beat just about every one of them with the help of the inmate paralegal, Law.

The chief informed Mr. Graves that if he wanted to go after Snake he has to be right and exact.

"You're gonna need a snake to catch this Snake," He told Mr. Graves.

The chief ordered special detail officers to search the housing unit Snake were living on. Snake's cell was particularly searched for secret exits. None were found. The maintenance crew and locksmith examined the hatch leading to the top of the cells in the unit. Cell bars prevented access to the top, which was connected to a hatch door.

A thick brass key was used to open the hatch door. Once the door was opened, a sensor beam triggered an alarm in Center Control. The hatch door was checked daily, and recorded by a computer. The officers climbed through the hatch and searched the top of the cells, finding no weapons, reporting their search results to Mr. Graves. All of the chief's usual inmate informants had no information on Snake's weapon sales. Muscleman only sold to those who were close to him. The chief told Mr. Graves the boy was lying about Snake. But Mr. Graves kept the theory in his mind, "You got to use a snake to catch a Snake."

CHAPTER 6

Mr. Graves discussed a job opportunity with his brother Leroy, so that he could work for him, temporarily as his executive assistant. Leroy served nineteen years at Trenton State Prison as an inmate for armed robbery. He received no early release for good behavior, because his behavior was never good. His nickname in prison was Havoc. During his time in Trenton State, he either argued with the officers or fought with them.

Leroy hated cops on the street and corrections officers in prison. He was one of the most indocile inmates at this prison. He'd been released from prison shortly after his brother Mr. Grave began to work there. The executive assistant position has been vacant for three months. It was a liaison position between inmates and the administration. The inmates at the prison always consulted with the executive assistant about their issues with officers. And the administration told the executive assistant what issues he wanted him to tell the inmates.

Mr. Graves refused to hire anyone for this position because he wanted the inmates to write or address him with their problems. He didn't need a go-between man; he wanted to be the man. Leroy was well known throughout the prison population and was despised by officers. His last housing unit was the same unit Snake lived in. Leroy knew where all of the hiding spots were because he hid many illegal drugs and weapons in that same housing unit. He also knew all of the snitches in that unit and throughout the prison.

Leroy was well qualified for the job as being a snake and he knew how to run a prison, but in an illegal way. Mr. Graves visited Leroy as he sat on his porch at his home. They stood on the front porch as Mr. Graves eagerly and impatiently forced his ideal on his brother. His brother told Leroy, that the task would be difficult for him. Because of the animosity the officers have for Leroy and the dislike that the officers have for Mr. Graves, forty-five to sixty days was all of the time he could give to him before the major complaints came. Leroy was in no hurry to go back to prison, especially the one he just left. Working in one was never on his mind and was out of the question. But his brother had special plans for him, and was determined to hire him.

"So all I have to do is find a sword and that's it. Can't you just get somebody to make you one in there, and hide it somewhere. So when the news media come, act like you just found it and give them a good speech. That will work little brother."

"It's not just about a sword. It's about finding out what's happening inside my prison, too. You know. Walk around the prison and find out what's going on inside. Socialize with the inmates. Like the ones you used to talk to in there."

Leroy wasn't trying to hear that and asked, "Don't you talk to the inmates in there? Or, are all of those inmates your enemies?"

Mr. Graves thought about it for a minute and told him, "You can relate to them better than I can because you know them better than I do." Mr. Graves became more specific as he told Leroy, "See, you know who the real snitches are, and who's selling the drugs in the prison. Plus you'll be getting paid for it, and this will look good on your resume. This would be a good way to rehabilitate yourself and get back into the work field, you feel me. I've already talked to the governor to give you a pardon. He's doing that as we speak. And when this job is done, I'll get in contact with some people to get you another job paying big bucks. With that pardon, it would be as if you never had a criminal record. As if you've never went to prison. So they have to hire you, you feel me. So look out for me big brother, please." After the pep talk, Leroy agreed to work for his brother with the promise to remain nonviolent. But that promise remained to be seen.

Darell was found not guilty and released from lockup. The state attorney general had no witnesses to contradict his story. And the alleged victim had a history of assaulting little boys. The weapons charge was also dropped although it was not determined for sure as yet who gave him the shank.

To prevent further attacks of Darell, Mr. Graves transferred him to the south part of the prison where no sex offenders were housed. Tomahawk and Law were still puzzled by Darell, as to who he was and why he confessed to the murder. Tomahawk wanted to meet him to also clarify his parental status with his new son. The south side of prison was basically isolated from the rest of the prison. It was difficult and almost impossible for these two to meet and socialize. Law was the go-between man with the two of them. He had access throughout the prison, doing legal work. "Legal work" was always his excuse to get inside of a housing unit.

Law walked to Darell's housing unit to deliver a message from Tomahawk. The officer in the unit directed him to Darell's cell. They stood outside his door and talked. After shaking his hand and giving him a half hug, he gave him job offers from the boss.

"Your pop sent me over to first congratulate you and welcome you out of lockup. And he wants to give you a job of your choice. I suggest that you work in the cookhouse, so you can get your eat on. Or you can work in the commissary so you won't have to buy smokes or deodorant and things like that.

"Is Tomahawk the warden now? Is he in charge of giving jobs out now?"

"No, it's not like that. See, you pick a job. See, this is how we do here. You pick a job that you want. If there's no opening for that position, Tomahawk and his boys will determine who should quit. So they'll tell them to quit. And if they don't quit, they'll get beaten up until their convinced that they shouldn't work there any more."

"Oh, that's how y'all do it?" Darell asked.

"It's the American way. You ain't know?"

Darell shook his head and asked, "Even if somebody wanted your job?"

"I'm exempted from all of that. Can't nobody handle my job, Young Man."

"Well if y'all doing it like that, I need y'all on the streets to look out for me like this, too."

"Yeah, but keep this on the low. You looked out for Tomahawk, so he's gonna look out for you."

"Well, if it's like that, get me a job where I can be around some females, yo. Are there any females in the kitchen? What you call it? The cookhouse?"

"It's a couple of men we can turn into females for you."

Darell started laughing.

"You serious with this, yo? I'm talking about some natural born females. The ones that look good and smell good. I ain't trying to get comfortable with these men in here. I ain't trying to lose my reputation."

"I'll get you in the infirmary where all the pretty nurses are."

"That's good money. That'll work. When do I start?"

"Give me about a week. I'll let you know something by then."

Law feels comfortable enough with him to ask Darell something personal. He stepped closer to Darell and asked, "Why did you confess to the murder?"

Darell shrugged his shoulders asking him, "Who had a better chance of being found not guilty?"

"Hey! What's you mom's name? Is she from Trenton?"

Darell smiled at him, and put his right fist up to his mouth, knowing Law wants to know if Tomahawk is really his father.

"All right. Write this down, yo. June twenty-first of last year. Get the newspaper article, either one of the Trenton papers, and read about me. My pop died that day, and I'm just trying to find his killer."

Law wrote the date down and looked at Darell to see if he was lying. Darell became agitated as he thought about his father. After shaking hands again, Law left the unit. Tomahawk felt relieved that there was no new son in his life. Getting Darell a job wasn't hard to do, because in some prisons only the strong survive. They decided to push up on an inmate who just started working in the infirmary. His brother was a corrections officer in another state prison. He received enough threats to know that he wasn't safe working outside of his housing unit.

That inmate ran to code 50 (medical emergency) calls, picking up beaten up inmates a number of times. When word went out that someone was going to get gotten, they usually got it. When the inmate quit his infirmary job, Law put Darell's paperwork in for the job. A week later, Darell started working the afternoon shift. The job took his mind off of the prison time he had to do. Working in the infirmary was his first job as a man, but unfortunately, it's in prison. That went against what his father told him where not to go.

The beauty of the nurses and working with doctors plus the excitement with the job was fine with him. He wore white pants, white medical shirts, and black shiny shoes. Everyday before he went to work, he brushed his shoes. The inmate barber gave him a small bottle of aftershave in exchange for bandages.

Terry, the man who murdered his father, was transferred to a hospital outside of the prison. He was housed in the same medical unit Darell was working in, but got transferred out because his health condition became worse.

Terry was dying with AIDS and tuberculosis. He had a weak heart and was in need of plenty of medication.

Prison medical staff wanted him to be in a better medical facility to receive advanced treatment, so they transferred him to a hospital until his condition improved a little.

Law located Darell and gave him newspaper copies of the incident with Terry. Law told him he saw Terry in prison but forgot where Terry was housed. He promised to get back to Darell with that information.

Mr. Graves' brother, Leroy, started his new job as an executive assistant, wearing a suit and tie, trying to look professional. He had access to the whole prison; talking to any and every inmate he walked up to. All of the officers that knew him as an inmate gave him a hard time whenever they approached him. After Leroy transferred out of the prison, the officers were told that Leroy was the one who assaulted his housing unit officer, leaving the officer unconscious. When he wanted to go through doors, they made him wait longer, by taking their time opening the doors or gates as he stood there.

Some officers attempted to provoke him into fighting them, the same way he used to provoke them. But Leroy was on a mission, so he kept his composure. He avoided his old housing unit because of the confrontation he'd had with the housing unit officer. It wasn't really a confrontation; it was actually an assault. Leroy punched the officer on the side of the head, knocking the officer unconscious. The officer didn't know who or what hit him, but was informed a week later by Snake that it was Leroy who punched him. Leroy went home four days after the assault, and was never charged.

The housing unit in the west side of the prison was the same unit Snake lived in. Leroy knew Snake but never trusted him. Leroy refused to even speak to Snake. Snake always indulged in illegal activities and never seemed to get caught. Leroy thought Snake was a snitch, which was the reason why he kept his distance from him.

Four weeks went by and Snake's name wasn't connected in any way to any illegal sales of drugs or weapons. One inmate informed Leroy that Snake told the officer Leroy punched him. All of Leroy's connections told him Snake had been going to church services and praising the Lord. But Leroy knew that church was just a front for

Snake. They said Snake was up for parole in about three weeks. Leroy put word out to Snake that he was going to step to him with a vengeance for telling on him, before his job was completed at the prison. Leroy knew that church services were one of the areas that the inmates discussed their illegal activities. Leroy attended church service one Sunday and was shocked to see so many atheistic inmates who attended services that day.

Leroy talked to Muscleman after services, and commended him for trying to seek some divine help to change his illegal ways. Muscleman the Hustleman always attended services to conduct business. He told Leroy before he left that the preacher had a hustle too. The preacher man hustled with the Bible, and gets paid for reading the words in it.

"My hustle is anything I can get my hands on, except the Bible. If Jehovah God, Buddha, Jesus or any other god wants me to be rich, they'll see to it that I'll get my riches," Hustleman told him. "Who ever made me is going to see to it that I get rich. Watch, my time will come. You'll see."

Leroy looked around the chapel after the service to see where he would hide a sword. The podium was the only place a sword could fit. Leroy's celebrity status with the inside population was mixed at the prison. Some inmates looked at Leroy as one of them, while the others looked at him as a part of the administration. Leroy was locked up at the prison, fighting correction officers as a rebel, so the inmates felt he understood their anger and pain.

The inmate known as Snake, one of the most popular and notorious prisoners in the prison, despised Leroy. Snake envied Leroy and hated his brother, Mr. Graves, too. Leroy made his usual rounds through the prison, wearing one of his finest suits as he walked, enjoying his day when he was approached by Snake in a disrespectful manner.

"Hey! Hey! Hey! Leroy!" Snake called to him as he walked up to him.

"You can call me Mr. Graves," Leroy told him.

"Yeah. That's right. Because you're Mr. Executive Assistant wearing Italian suits and alligator shoes," Snake told him with attitude.

"Leroy!" he called him again. "What's this about you putting word out that you're gonna get me with a vengeance because I told the officer you punched him?"

"I keeps my word. You did what you had to do. Now I'll do what I got to do."

Snake smiled and said, "So you and your punk brother gonna jump me? I got people up in here, too. You gonna need your whole family, Leroy, to get with me."

Leroy started taking off his jacket, feeling that this was a good opportune time to get revenge on Snake for telling on him.

"Let's do this. We don't need my brother."

Snake looked behind him at the officers, and thought about his parole and told him, "Look around you, fool. If we start fighting here, who do you think these officers are gonna jump on first?"

Leroy thought about it, knowing that the officers hated him, so he put his jacket back on.

"I'll find another way to get a snake."

"I'm paroled next month, Leroy. Maybe we can battle on the blocks."

Leroy responded, "I'll get with you one way or another," and walked away.

While walking, Snake shouted to him, "You can tell your punk brother I ain't got no love for him either."

Leroy ignored him and continued to walk. That afternoon, Leroy discussed that encounter with his brother. From that discussion, Mr. Graves became vexed and decided to get back at Snake, for disrespecting the family.

The next day, Monday, Mr. Graves ordered two officers Crusher and Bad News to escort Snake to the famous understanding room, the same interview room Darell was in when he understood why he shouldn't lie to Mr. Graves.

When asked about his sword, Snake told Mr. Graves he didn't have one. He swore that he was a man of God. Mr. Graves left them in the room. He ordered his brother to search Snake's housing unit. Leroy requested for a corrections lieutenant and a maintenance man to walk with him.

Almost all of the inmates in the housing unit left for work or went out to the yard that morning for recreation. Snake was in the interview room. The Lieutenant ordered the housing unit officer not to let any inmates enter the unit.

Leroy refused to speak to the officer he punched and walked into the unit's closet. His old housing unit looked like a modernized dungeon. It was kept clean and painted bright blue. The brass in the unit was always shining. Leroy walked with his crew around his old housing unit looking at the walls, steps, and windowpanes.

He walked up to the fourth tier with his crew. Leroy looked through the black painted iron bars above his head that lead to the top of the cells. As they walked to the end of the tier, Leroy glanced inside of Snake's cell. They reached the end of the tier and stared at the locked hatch door that leads to the top of the cells.

"The key for the lock is in Center Control," the lieutenant told him.

"We were up here last week talking about this door," the maintenance man said smiling.

"And if you did go through that hatch, an alarm in Center Control would go off."

Leroy asked the lieutenant if he could search Snake's cell. The lieutenant gave him some rubber gloves and ordered the officer to open Snake's cell door. Once inside, Leroy walked to the back of the cell. He noticed no escape routes. Leroy picked up Snake's personal property and came across a toothbrush with dry black paint on it. Leroy looked around the cell again and noticed nothing in the cell with black paint on it.

He remembered seeing the black bars above his head outside of the cell, and decided to look at it again. Out of all of the years that he'd been in this unit, he never saw any officer checking these bars with a rubber mallet. The mallet that was supposed to be used for checking the bars stayed in the officer's desk. The hatch door was out of the question. Leroy began to think as an inmate again.

As inmates, they knew that they had to manipulate or circumvent all mechanical devices. Leroy walked downstairs and returned with a broom. As he walked back down the top tier, he hit every iron bar with the broom. Five bars were knocked loose by the broom and dropped to the floor in front of Snake's cell. Small magnets placed on the top ends of the bars held these loose bars in place.

The lieutenant and maintenance man stared at the sawed off bars on the floor. Leroy pulled the trashcan down the tier to the gap in the bars, turned it upside down and climbed up on it, and went through the hole. The maintenance man and lieutenant followed him. Standing on top of the cells looking around, Leroy asked them, "Where would you hide a sword?"

The first instinct of an officer in an isolated area or new institution is to look for a breach in security. The first instinct of an inmate in a new or different institution was to look for a place to stash something valuable or important to them. As they stood on top of Snake's cell, Leroy looked at the insulation wrapped around an iron hot pipe. This pipe was three inches away from the electrical wires on the wall. He asked the maintenance man for his utility knife.

The duct tape wrapped around the insulation had staples in it and was painted over. After cutting through the insulation, Leroy and the maintenance man pulled the insulation from the pipe. A two-foot bed slab that was made into a sword was placed upright against this pipe. It was sharpened on both sides and had a cloth grip. The slab was from the old beds that had been in the prison seventy or eighty years ago. The pieces of metal weren't too hard to break off. The inmates would place a metal stinger on both ends of the metal and plug the stinger into the electrical socket. These stingers would melt the slab, as they got hotter. As the slab melted, the inmate stood on top of the slab until it broke off. These are the same stingers the inmates use to heat up their coffee or tea, when they place the metal stinger in the cup. The lieutenant called Mr. Graves and asked him to meet him in the understanding room. Snake was still in the room with the two escorting officers Bad News and Crusher standing by the door. By way of radio Lieutenant Smith gave Mr. Graves the signal that he found the sword. "Lieutenant Smith to Mr. Graves . . ."

"This is Mr. Graves. Go Lieutenant."

"Be advised, I have a delivery for you. It's a boy."

Mr. Graves walked back into the interview room, sat in front of Snake and asked him again about the sword.

"Do you have any shanks or weapons that I should know about?"

"No, Mr. Graves. I'm trying to get paroled out of here. I ain't got any shanks. I told you I ain't about that," Snake told him with an honest look on his face. Snake knew that his cell and maybe his housing unit were being searched. Mr. Graves wouldn't have him sitting in the understanding room if they weren't being searched. He also knew that the top of his cell was searched a week ago without the sword being found by the officers that searched for it. Snakes confidence grew a little stronger after Mr. Graves asked him again about the sword. Feeling sure that it will never be found, he produced a little smile on his face. As they sat at the table, Lieutenant Smith walked in the door and held it open. The maintenance man walked in next. Snake turned to look at Mr. Graves and smiled, thinking that his sword wasn't found. Mr. Graves looked away from Snake and gently smiled as Leroy walked into the room with the weapon, holding the ends of it with gloves on his hands. Snake's smiled dropped from his face, wondering what Mr. Graves was smiling at. Snake turned in his chair toward the door and saw Leroy displaying the weapon, with a smile on his face. Snake's mouth dropped open. He felt betrayed and shocked, as he remembered Leroy's statement about getting back at him. Snake looked back at Mr. Graves and at the two officers, and then he began to run toward the door.

"Get him!" Mr. Graves shouted.

After this incident, Trenton State Prison officials had one less shank to worry about.

CHAPTER 7

Darell never knew the impact that his words about the sword to Mr. Graves had on the institution. All he knew at that time was in order for him to save himself; someone else had to be sacrificed. His mission at the prison took his mind off his ten year sentence. The infirmary job kept him occupied, and satisfied to be around so many beautiful women. Darell kept in touch with his mom every day, even thanking her for her guidance.

He never would have imagined the importance of bagging up and taking out trash, if she hadn't instilled it in him. Being a hospital porter enabled him to understand what it felt like to have a job. Cleaning up and taking out garbage was his number one priority. That was what he looked forward to, and did everyday.

"Excuse me, Nurse. Do you want me to empty that trash can for you?" Or "Officer, can I dump your trash can?" Those were his everyday words at work. All of the nurses grew to like him, and he was feeling them, too. Officer Pat walked into Darell's self-made lounge and asked Darell who his father was and if his father and mother were together. Darell told her his father was murdered up the street that past summer. He told her the man ran after shooting his father and got hit by a car. He added, "But I'm still single." She smiled and walked away. Tomahawk was a distant memory to him, and was someone he hadn't officially met. Darell's mind was too occupied with work and listening to rap music in his cell, or writing rhymes. He made the Intensive Care Unit in the infirmary his lounge. The ICU was not occupied, so he relaxed in the chair and watched TV when his work was complete. He felt secure in his spot and well protected from the other inmates at the prison. Darell had the best inmate legal counsel protecting him legally, and one of the most fearsome inmates known throughout the prison, protecting him from bodily harm. Each day was a stress-free day.

All of that changed one afternoon at work when he checked into work. The nurses were complaining about an inmate in the ICU room. He heard them talking about the inmate complaining about everything. That inmate constantly pushed the nurse's attention buzzer, wanting to be pampered on demand.

The female officer, Pat, who worked in the infirmary, became disgusted with this inmate. She cussed him out and told him not to call her for anything else. After leaving his room, she refused to go see what his complaints were anymore. That was the same inmate whose condition had gotten worse and was transferred to an outside hospital. He complained before while he was there, now he continued his complaints now that he's back.

The nurse asked Darell to accompany her to the ICU room. Someone that was really in need of medical attention now occupied Darell's self-made lounge. As he entered his former lounge, Darell saw a man lying on the bed with tubes protruding from his nose. A heart monitor was next to the bed with wires attached to his chest. His left arm and both legs were paralyzed.

Darell took three steps toward him and stopped. The nurse walked to the monitor and checked his vital signs. The man that killed Darell's father was now dependent on him for comfort. Darell was shocked to see Terry, but felt satisfied to know he had been found.

Terry asked for two more pillows and some water.

"Get me another blanket. They got that air conditioner up too high," he complained to the nurse.

Terry looked at Darell and asked, "Why you standing over there like you gonna catch something from me?"

Chills covered Darell's body to a point where his body felt frozen. The nurse asked him to get another blanket, but he couldn't move. Terry didn't recognize who Darell was and didn't really care. Darell wanted to black out on him but didn't know how or where to start.

"Boy, are you deaf? Get me another blanket from out that closet. It's cold in here," Terry said arrogantly.

Darell looked at the nurse before turning to walk out of the room. The blanket reminded him of how his father was covered with a blanket after he died. Now this man wanted Darell to give him a blanket to make him feel comfortable.

"Where you going? The closet is over here, boy." He heard Terry say as he walked out.

Officer Pat saw him walking toward her with tears in his eyes. He walked right past her without saying a word. Darell walked into an empty room and started crying. Officer Pat went into Terry's room and asked the nurse if everything was all right. Afterward, she talked to Darell about the medical unit.

"Don't feel sorry for that inmate. You're going to see inmates in worst conditions than that. They should've given you a class or something to prepare you for this. Wait until you start seeing blood, or their brains hanging out of their heads. That's when it's going to start bothering you. What you just saw wasn't nothing. Having tubes in your nose and wires on you ain't nothing. That's average down here, so get used to it." She stared at him as she shook her head from side to side, thinking he was going to quit.

"When you see or come across something you're not sure of, or you can't handle, just say a prayer or something. I'll call your officer and tell him you're coming back. Stay in this room and get yourself together before you leave. Take your time and I'll see you back here tomorrow, if you don't quit."

She walked out and closed the door behind her, not knowing the real reason behind his pain. Seeing Terry once again brought back bad memories of his father's death. Carrying out revenge wasn't as easy as planned for Darell. There wouldn't be any self-defense excuses. This time it would be straight-up murder. The peculiar part about that was Darell was charged and labeled as a murderer twice. Yet he didn't know what it felt like to murder someone.

Terry took all of the enthusiasm and fun out of coming to work. While at work, Darell avoided his former lounge, the ICU room, as much as possible. Since Terry was in the condition he was in, he wasn't going anywhere anytime soon. Darell decided to put a pillow over his face and smother him the next time Terry asked for one.

But then, he thought that would be too painless. Beating him with the broomstick would be the better choice, he thought. While thinking about it, he wanted Terry to bleed the same way his father bled to death. So with that thought Darell needed a shank.

There were plenty of sharp scissors in the infirmary area. No need for Muscleman the Hustleman's assistance. All he needed, as he learned from inmate Two-for-One at the reception unit, was some chewing gum. So he kept a pack in his pocket at all times.

The opportunity for Darell to use his gum came when the medical staff ran to a medical emergency. The nurse used nine-inch scissors to cut medical tape on an inmate who had been in a fight and cut by other inmates. The nurses pulled out bandages, medical tape, gauze, scissors, towels, and peroxide from their grab bag. Darell took the opportunity to pick up the nine-inch scissors with the bright orange handle. He held it underneath his white long-sleeved shirt with his fingers.

After they patched the inmate up as best they could, they escorted the inmate to the infirmary. When Officer Pat walked into the holding room to get the inmate's name and state number, Darell stashed the scissors. He took pieces of his chewing gum out of his mouth and placed it along the scissors. Inmate Two-for-One said to place "big pieces on it, to make sure it sticks."

With the gum on the scissors, Darell placed the scissors on the bottom of the officers' desk. The scissors weren't discovered missing until the end of the shift when all of the equipment was counted.

That was the only scissors with an orange handle on it, and the longest pair too. Every inmate hospital porter was searched. The next day a search team of corrections officers searched the whole prison.

The next day, prior to going to work, Darell packed up all of his personal property. He wasn't planning on returning to his cell, and didn't really care. Although he knew that all of his property would be searched by corrections officers, Darell neatly placed his property in boxes and set them aside against the wall. Hoping that this will give them an idea of how they should replace his belongings back into the boxes after their search for any contraband, especially weapons. While at work he remained calm doing his casual duties in the infirmary. Terry's condition has gotten worst again. Now he was paralyzed all over from the neck down.

Darell did not want to quit work and did not want to cater to his enemy anymore. So he waited until Officer Pat was relieved for her break to remind Terry who he was. About four o'clock, she was relieved for break by a rookie officer. She walked outside to the front of the prison to smoke and get some fresh air.

Darell's housing unit officer was standing next to her talking to her outside as they smoked. Also, the superintendent, Mr. Graves, was on his way home as he left the building. He walked out of the building, and walked towards Darell's housing unit officer, smiled at him and said, "Is your inmate count right?"

His statement was in reference to an incorrect count this officer reported to center yesterday. Darell's housing officer always added Darell to his count whenever Darell was at work. The officer who relieved him reported in another count and reported Darell missing. Being a senior officer, he should've known that rookies always go by the book.

As Mr. Graves exited the parking lot, he looked at the prison's biggest parking lot. It was nearly vacant and scheduled to be paved tomorrow. But one car was parked all the way in the back of this lot. He drove through the emptied parking lot to the vehicle. There were four notice fliers on the windshield about the scheduled paving.

The vehicle was a dusty and dirty black S-Class Benz. Mr. Graves walked around the car to look at the temporary tag on the back window. He saw the name Darell Steps on it and began to wonder where he'd heard that name before. He decided to check the employee sheet the next day.

When Officer Pat's relief officer left the desk and made his rounds in the infirmary, Darell removed the scissors from under the desk and placed it inside of his long-sleeved shirt. He held the scissor against his wrist by pressing his fingers against his sleeve, holding the weapon in place. The officer returned to the desk, and Darell cautiously walked to the linen closet and grab the thickest wool blanket, that was on the shelf. He tucked the scissors inside of his pants and held the scissors against his waist by pressing the blanket against his shirt, prior to visiting Terry in the ICU. Darell entered the room and closed the door behind him, with his back pressing against the door. After taking a deep breath, Darell removed his weapon from his waist, and walked over to Terry with the scissors in his right hand. With hate and revenge in his heart, he threw the blanket on the floor next to the bed, and stood on the left side of Terry as he slept.

After thinking about his father for a few seconds, he said a short prayer, raised the scissors over his head, and above Terry's heart. Pausing in this position for about fifteen seconds, he realized that this was not the man his father wanted him to be. With tears in his eyes, Darell slowly lowered the scissors and placed them on Terry's chest. They lay on top of his heart with the pointed sharpened edge pointing toward Terry's face.

Officer Pat and Darell's housing unit officer commented on what Mr. Graves said about the count. Officer Pat asked him, "Did you tell the other officer where Darell was before you left?"

"Yeah, I'm straight this time. But he should've just relieved me and sat down and relaxed yesterday. He didn't have to count those inmates over again like that. That made me look bad."

"He's new at this. That's what they teach them at the academy," Officer Pat said.

As they continued smoking, Darell's officer told her, "I'm surprised they didn't call an escape on Darell."

As he thought further he said, "Hey! I saw him somewhere before. His face looks familiar. I first thought Darell was my cousin, but my people said that they don't know him. But I know I've seen him somewhere before."

"He's from Trenton. He's from out Wilbur section," Officer Pat told him.

"Oh, okay. Maybe I know his father then. I probably know his father if I see him."

"Well, you're not gonna see his father no time soon. The man's dead. Darell said somebody shot him and ran across the street and got hit by a car while trying to get away. He got shot right up the street."

"Last year? When was this? Last year? Right up the street?" he asked with excitement.

"I hit the guy who ran across the street. That was me who hit him. That was um . . . that was um . . . what's his face. You know him . . . um," He said as he tapped his foot on the ground. "That was um . . . Terry. Yeah, that was Terry who ran. He ran right into my car. Right after work."

"You mean Terry in the infirmary?" she asked hoping for a different Terry.

"Yeah, that's him. The one that can't move, looking all ugly in the face."

"Terry killed Darell's father?" she asked out loud.

"Do Darell know Terry killed his father?"

Simultaneously, they thought about the missing scissors and looked at each other with their mouths wide open. They threw their cigarettes on the ground and ran back inside the prison.

Terry opened his eyes from sleeping and saw Darell standing on the left side of him.

"What's your problem?" he asked.

"You." Darell responded as he stared at him with hate in his eyes. Terry glanced at his chest and looked at the tip of the scissors pointing toward him.

"Why you put them scissors on me for?"

"I was gonna put them in your heart. But I wanted to wake you up first, before I cut your heart out, Yo."

"Boy, you must have lost your mind. Didn't your father teach you about playing with pointy things?" Darell kept his composure as he told him,

"No, he didn't get to that part. He was going to tell me a lot of things about life . . . before you killed him."

Darell looked at the door for a second and back at Terry.

"I'm the one who chased you across the street before you got hit by that car."

Officer Pat called the area sergeant as he stood next to the water fountain, and told him to follow her, as she ran with Darell's housing unit officer to the south entrance of the prison. The north entrance was a shorter distance, but it was temporarily shut down for cleaning. They couldn't get through the second security door because the metal detector kept going off on them. The three of them had to clear the machine before the officer standing on the other side of the other door could open it.

As Terry reflected on what Darell said, he remembered being chased and running, the day the car hit him. As Darell continued to talk, sweat began to flow down Terry's face from his head.

"I should cut your ears off, and shove them down your throat."

Terry looked at the emergency button to call the nurse, but couldn't move. He's paralyzed from the neck down and having problems breathing, too.

"What? You want me to push the button for you. Ha, Ha. Picture that. Take this pain like a man. Oh! I forgot. You can't feel anything below your neck, my bad." He moved closer to Terry's face and told him,

"When you go back to sleep, I'm gonna put this pillow over your face so you can't breathe. And while I'm smothering you, I'll be punching you in your face, you feel me."

Terry's heart started pumping faster as sweat poured down his face, as if he was in a marathon race.

Officer Pat, Sergeant Johnson and Darell's housing officer cleared the first security door in the south part of the prison. They ran toward the next security post and had to wait for the next officer to let them in. But he was not in sight. Central Control saw them on camera as they ran and called Sergeant Johnson by radio. They asked him if something was wrong. He said he didn't know and told them to stand by.

The heart monitor machine connected to Terry was beeping faster and faster. Terry's heart was pounding harder out of fear. He was gasping for air as Darell stood by his side planning his death.

"Or I might get Tomahawk to come in here and break you up first. Yeah and when he's finished with you, I'll cut your toes off with these scissors and stuff them in your mouth. I'll make you suffer the same way you made my father suffer."

Officer Pat and her fellow officers finally got past the last door before the infirmary. As they raced down the hallway, Terry went into a convulsion out of fear. He couldn't breathe and the beeping monitor made one long sound. The monitor was connected to the nurses' station and to Central Control. When Terry's heart stopped, the alarm activated.

Central Control announced a code 50 (Medical Emergency) in the infirmary over the intercom and radio. Officer Pat stopped running and said out loud holding her head, "Oh! My God!"

The sergeant stopped running, too, as he watched Officer Pat. Sergeant Johnson finally figured out why he was running and called Central Control on the radio.

"Sergeant Johnson to Central Control. We have a code 50 in the infirmary."

"Central Control to Sergeant Johnson."

"Sergeant Johnson. Go, Central."

"We already know that, Sarge."

One of the on duty nurses snatched the grab bag with medical supplies in it off the table, and ran into the I.C.U. room. Officer Pat with her fellow officers came into the first of two doors of the infirmary. As the nurse entered Terry's room, she grabbed the cart with the defibrillator on it by the door, and pushed it to Terry. Darell was still standing on the other side of the bed watching.

She turned the machine on, grabbed the two prods, and stared at the scissors on Terry's chest. The nurse realized that the scissors were the ones she had been accused of losing, and was being threatened to be fired over. As the alarm continued to sound, she stood there wondering where the scissors came from and why they were on his chest. She glances at Darell while forgetting about Terry, as if he didn't even existed. She than glanced back at Terry, and remembered why she ran into this room. The nurse snatched the scissors off of his chest, and threw them on the floor behind her.

Officer Pat ran into the room as the scissors slid toward her, hitting her left foot. She looked at the scissors, picked them up and looked at Darell. As the nurse placed the two prods on Terry's chest, Darell's body trembled as the electrical currents lift Terry's lifeless body off the bed.

The second nurse entered the room and shouted, "Hit him again!"

The second hit again raised Terry's back off the bed. She increased the voltage and hit him one more time with the prod. There was no pulse. Darell stared at the body with tears in his eyes. His housing unit officer escorted him out of the room. While standing on the outside of the room, Darell was ordered by his officer to put his hands up on the window. With legs spread and both of his hands raised up on the window, Darell's housing unit officer thoroughly searched him for more weapons. As he searched him, Darell watched as the nurse picked up the blanket from the floor and slowly covered Terry's body with the wool blanket, starting with his feet.

CHAPTER 8

The next morning, Mr. Graves figured it all out. His conclusion was Darell parked his car in the prison's parking lot before he came into the prison to seek revenge. Once again Darell was placed back in lockup. Looking out of the window that time, the only vehicle he saw in the prison's parking lot that was to be paved was a black Benz.

Darell remembered walking in that direction with his father, when his father gave him the keys to his new black Benz, with chrome rim wheels on it.

"That's my car!" he said out loud, as he hit the right side of his fist against the window. He broke down in tears behind these walls, feeling hurt and frustrated. Not only could he not get to his car, he also knows that he disappointed his father's wishes, by being locked up in prison. Darell began to realize that this is not a positive way to represent, or to emulate his father. He thought about how proud his father was of him, when he received those keys. While staring out the window with tears in his eyes, he also thought about all of the letters he received from his mother, about how proud she was that he finally has a job working in prison, teaching him how to be a responsible man. And about how proud she is with his behavior, by obeying the laws in prison as a man. Now he's wondering if his mom will still believe in him, after he wrote her back, telling her that he made a positive change in his life.

Law requested to defend Darell, knowing that his case was an impossible case to win. The Attorney General's office refused to give leniency to inmates unless they were snitches. Mr. Graves didn't believe in leniency and did not tolerate or negotiate with murderers.

Law wanted to do the unthinkable. He decided to put Mr. Graves on the defense, and to appeal to Mr. Graves' conscience. Law knew Mr. Graves thought he was going to come with the usual defense, or try to make a deal with him. So Law switched the whole defense up and asked that Mr. Graves put in a request to the Governor of New Jersey to pardon Darell. He heard about the pardon Mr. Graves got for his brother Leroy, so why not get another one for his client Darell. Law and Mr. Graves argued in the understanding room for over three hours about Darell. No one compromised.

"That was a premeditated murder. That boy knew what he wanted to do before he got here. The bold part about it is, he parked his car in my parking lot before making this his home."

"There were no stab wounds, Mr. Graves, so there wasn't a murder."

"The nurse's report says the boy placed that weapon on his chest. That constitutes a threat in my book. And if a man is threatened like that and dies of a heart attack, that's a fourth degree murder. We didn't charge him with killing that other inmate. He's got to pay for this one."

"He was attacked by that child rapist." Law stated.

Mr. Graves stood up, placed both of his fists on the table, leaned forward toward Law and said, "So the paralyzed man attacked him this time, too? I don't think so."

"Let's just look at all of the possible things he could have done to him." Law began to examine all of the possibilities. "Darell could've beaten the man to death. He could've poisoned him or smothered him. He had the opportunity to stab him. He didn't do any of that. Darell is not a murderer."

"So now all of the young thugs think they can come to my prison seeking revenge and you find that acceptable?"

"Mr. Graves, this is a unique and personal situation. There was no bloodshed. Darell is still young and does have a heart and feelings. From what I was told, his father parked the car in the parking lot. They were on their way to the car."

"So now you want me to get him a pardon?"

"He looks at you as a father figure. He even helped you catch a snake. An inmate that despised you, and your family."

"That boy was going to talk one way or another. He had no choice but to give up Snake." Mr. Graves stated as he reminisced on how he forced Darell to talk.

"Mr. Graves, the boy is young and just starting out in life. He doesn't need to be here. This would be the only pardon from this prison in years. The only family he has is his mom. Consider his pardon please."

"I might consider making him a deal, only because it was his father, Terry killed. But let it be known in my prison, revengeful acts will not be tolerated. He got his revenge, and now he has to pay for it. That's how I feel about it. It's a wrap."

"Darell sought revenge for his father . . . not for someone just off the blocks, like a friend or neighbor, Mr. Graves."

"Vengeance is mine, said the Lord."

Mr. Graves told that to Law as he opened the desk drawer, pulled out a pen, glanced at a Bible in that drawer and took that out too.

"Maybe you can be a father figure to him, and teach that young boy that. You probably never heard about that, huh, Mr. Law. It's in the Bible."

Mr. Graves placed the bible on the desk in front of him.

Law had a loss for words. He felt defeated in this case. Darell's case was the only case that he personally cared about and he was losing it right from the start.

"Yes, I heard about that, Mr. Graves. But let's use the Bible and compare the two." Law stood up and began to preach as if he was a defense attorney in court.

"A young man is being charged with murder, just because he stood next to a dying man. No stab wounds. No physical bruises and no asphyxiation. He is accused of murdering a man that committed murder. A man that robbed people. A man who stole from many people. A man that had no respect for the laws in society on the streets. No respect for prison law or institution law, no respect for the staff members, nurses, or officers here in prison. Which means, he didn't even have respect for you. Terry had no respect for nobody's law. Not even God's law."

Mr. Graves turned toward his left, away from facing Law, and covered the right side of his face with his right hand, to indicate to Law that he wasn't interested in anything else that he had to say. Law ignored that gesture, and boldly walked around the table to face Mr. Graves, and picked the Bible up off the table. He held the book in his left hand, as he glided his right thumb across the edge of the pages to turn to a scripture. He decided to challenge Mr. Graves on God's law, in hopes that Mr. Graves would have a different prospective about God's law. Knowing that Mr. Graves has a very fast temper, Law felt as though he had nothing else to lose, even if it was his life.

"Romans 12:19. This is the scripture you're talking about. 'Vengeance is mine says the Lord.' They say that the Lord works in mysterious ways. Don't you agree with that, Mr. Graves?"

"Yes. The Lord has convinced me. I'm a believer of that."

"Then tell me something, Mr. Graves."

Law closed the bible and stared into Mr. Graves's eyes as he asked him, "Based on the lifestyle of Terry. Was Darell really responsible for Terry's death?"

As Law placed the Bible on the desk in front of Mr. Graves he asked,

"Or was the **Lord**?"

Those questions gave Mr. Graves something serious to contemplate on as he stared at the Bible in front of him.

On Thursday, Mr. Graves's brother, Leroy, completed his covert operations job, as an executive assistant. Although he enjoyed his job playing the role as a diplomat, he was used to fighting. That was what he did best. Leroy's last assignment was to visit Darell's mother, and hand deliver her a certified pardon letter from the office of the Governor of New Jersey, for Darell. All of Darell's criminal charges were expunged with that pardon. Leroy told her about Darell's Benz in the parking lot, and suggested that she get it washed before picking Darell up from the prison. The next day while at work in intake, Tomahawk completed his inmate processing assignments. The intake sergeant handed him a proclamation sheet, with a transfer paper attached to it. The paper had a gold seal on the letterhead with the words, Office of the Governor of New Jersey on it.

Darell Steps' name was on the proclamation. He received a full pardon. Tomahawk's job was to transfer him out of the prison as a free man.

Tomahawk had never seen a pardon before and he thought this was a joke. The door to his area opened with an officer and an inmate coming through. Tomahawk never met Darell, but heard about him and thought, "This might be him." The officer who was called Bad News by the inmates was ordered to escort Darell out of the prison, to prevent anymore restroom attacks. Tomahawk realized this was not a joke, as he stared in amazement. He couldn't believe how young he looked.

As Darell walked toward Tomahawk, his steps shortened and slowed when he saw him. Without saying a word, they looked at each other. Tomahawk reached out for Darell's right hand, grabbed it, shook it, and then gave him a half hug.

After the hug Tomahawk told him, "Stay strong out there."

Darell smiled back at him.

Tomahawk turned to the officer and told him, "I always knew one day, Bad News would come through here with some good news." Tomahawk laughed about that. Bad News didn't find any humor in that statement, so he walked past Darell and said, "Let's go."

As the officer opened the second door, Tomahawk shouted, "Hey! Darell!"

Darell turned toward him and heard Tomahawk say, "Thanks."

Darell smiled and walked out the door.

His mother waited across the street in his black Benz, receiving much attention from men that were trying to holla at her. After greeting her with a kiss and a hug, he opened the door to let his mother in the passenger's side. Darell turned to look at the prison feeling relieved and excited. While reflecting on his life behind those walls, a voice sounding like inmate Law hollered out of the barred window, "Darell!"

Still looking in that direction, but unable to see inside the window, Darell waved. While getting into the driver's side of the car, that same voice hollered, "I see you!" Darell smiled at him before driving away, leaving behind a memory.

www.ingramcontent.com/pod-product-compliance
Ingram Content Group UK Ltd.
Pitfield, Milton Keynes, MK11 3LW, UK
UKHW041930190726
13854UKWH00004B/1532

9 781425 773205